Richmond S. Dement

Napoleon and Josephine

A Tragedy in a Prologue and five Acts

Richmond S. Dement

Napoleon and Josephine
A Tragedy in a Prologue and five Acts

ISBN/EAN: 9783337349738

Printed in Europe, USA, Canada, Australia, Japan

Cover: Foto ©Andreas Hilbeck / pixelio.de

More available books at **www.hansebooks.com**

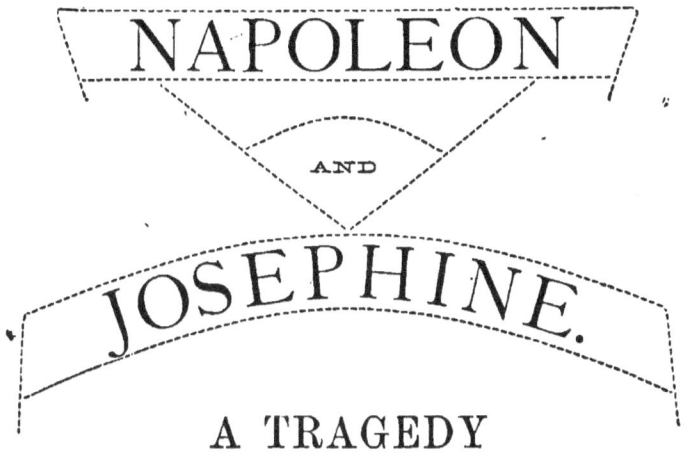

NAPOLEON

AND

JOSEPHINE.

A TRAGEDY

,IN

A PROLOGUE, AND FIVE ACTS,

BY

R. S. DEMENT.

AUTHOR'S EDITION.

CHICAGO:
LEGAL NEWS COMPANY.

1876.

AUTHOR'S PREFATORY NOTE.

In the theory that Napoleon was simply inspired by the belief that he was the child of destiny, there is hardly enough, to my mind, to reconcile the strange events and many inconsistencies of his remarkable career. I have therefore assumed that he was possessed of no less an hallucination than that, as the peculiar child of destiny, his course was directed, or rather *suggested*, by an actual presiding deity whom he personified as Fate. To her he conceived that he bore something of the same relation as Achilles to Thetis, though recognizing in Fate one possessed of no less power than Jove himself. I prefer the word *suggested*, as it is hardly in keeping with the character of Napoleon that he would have submitted to more than this even from the Immortals.

The affection of Napoleon for Josephine is proverbial, and it is hardly necessary for me to do

more than affirm that, perhaps, there is no recorded
instance of a higher or tenderer love between man
and wife, and yet, love—the strongest passion of
humanity, in which the soul reaches nearest to
the Infinite—was made to yield to what would certainly have been a lower incentive, had he not believed that all heaven and earth stood in waiting
for his action.

I have, it will be discovered, antedated and
crowded events, and entirely ignored many of the
most remarkable events and characters connected
with Napoleon's career.   To the Directors, Barras,
Gohier and Moulins, I have attributed all the con-
spiracies that appear in the play.   Eugene de
Béauharnais, whose age is advanced, did not return
with Junot and Joseph Bonaparte when the Standards and Bulletins were sent to the Directory, as
appears in the play.   These, and other obvious
deviations from historical accuracy will, it is trusted,
not diminish the pleasure the author hopes the
reader will find in this production.   In the main it
is true to history.

The author claims that the tragic ending of Act
V. is not far from the actual history of the death

of The Empress Josephine, for the divorce was certainly the death-knell of her happiness, and the cloud that first dimmed and finally obscured the star of Napoleon.

To secure as early publication as circumstances required, it was found necessary to omit the foot notes and appendix, in which due credit is given where the author feels indebted.

R. S. D.

DRAMATIS PERSONÆ.

Napoleon Bonaparte (the General of France);
    afterwards Emperor Napoleon I.
Eugene de Beauharnais.
Joseph Bonaparte.
Lucien Bonaparte.
Compte de Barras.
Carnot.
Gohier.
Moulins.
Larevilliere Lepeaux.
Letourneur.
Rewbell.
Ragideau.
Count von Coblentz.
Marquis Manfredini.
Reynard (a Soldier); afterwards Valet to the
    Emperor.
Officer of the Guard.
Augereau.
Oriani.
Le Gros.
Pope Pius VII.

Joseph Marie Rosa de Tacher de la Pagerie;
  afterwards
Viscountess de Beauharnais; *afterwards*
Empress Josephine.
Mary (sister of Josephine).
Princess Augusta.
Hortense de Beauharnais.
Euphemia (a Sybil).

1st, 2d and 3d Members of the Council of the
  Five Hundred.—1st and 2d Citizens.—1st,
  2d and 3d Secretaries.—Carbon.—St. Rejeant.—Limœlin.—A Little Girl.—Prelates.—Members of Bonaparte Family.—
  Lady Attendants.—Citizens.—Soldiers.—
  Courtiers.—Pages.—Negroes.

PROLOGUE.

MARTINIQUE.

A bower looking out upon the sea. Inland the background, at first undulating, rises to mountains.

Looking through the bower, the placid surface of the water is discovered sparkling in the sunlight, while at the entrance is suspended a silken hammock ornamented with flowers.

Upon the opening of the scene, is discovered a party of negroes in conversation.

Enter EUPHEMIA.

EUPHEMIA.

But yesterday a heavy sky !
The clouds hung dark and ominous o'erhead ;
To-day how beautiful !   And to-morrow—
Ah ! ah !

A NEGRO (*approaching*).
What have the stars to say for me ?

EUPHEMIA.

The stars are hid from mortal eyes to-day;
Too bright a sun shuts out the great beyond
No less than heavy clouds.

NEGRO.

                   Cannot you see
Beyond clouds or sun?

EUPHEMIA.

                  Ah! who can see
The great futurity?

NEGRO.

          Then I will go.

EUPHEMIA.

Stay! let me look into your hand—
A happy life awaits you, live in hope.
Only a few dark days, and then—

NEGRO.

                  What then?

EUPHEMIA.

Wait patiently and you shall see, shall see.
      [A young negress approaches. EUPHEMIA
          takes her hand, gazes into it. Then,
          without speaking, leads her to 1ST NE-
          GRO, *and, putting her hand in his*:
Your fates are one.

[*Whereupon all the negresses rush to have
their fortunes told. Old* EUPHEMIA
*throws up her hands, and, catching
sight of the approaching* JOSEPHINE,
[*Exeunt.*

Enter JOSEPHINE.

JOSEPHINE.

Fair sylvan bower! O, can there be beside thee,
So lovely a spot in all the realms of earth ?
What magic pow'r could give such beauty birth;
Such forms and colors exquisite provide thee?
Thou dreamy scene of happy childhood's vision;
Shrine of delights supreme! sublime elysium!

Beneath my feet thy richest carpets spread,
Of green and gold, with bright-hued flowers blend-
    ing ;
And, as each petal yields its silvery tips
Of morning dew, and opes its tiny lips
To drink the sunlight, sweetest fragrance sending
On every breath that rises from its bed ;
Celestial, then, the bird-songs overhead,
With Æol's softened cadences attending.

The heaven-kissing mountains rise behind thee,
O'er whose grand heights the sun first peeps to find
    thee,
Then rushes down in warm embrace to bind thee,

Divinely tinting ere he will resign thee.

On either side the enchanted woodland lies—
Old-fabled labyrinthine mysteries,
Home of bright fays and goblin histories.

Above, what grotesque shapes of beauty race
Through the ethereal azure depths of heaven!
And, as the orb of day sinks in the west,
Kissing the silv'ry wavelet's sparkling crest,
What crystal splendor to the sea is given!
What tints sublime, what matchless colors grace
Those glory-pictures of mysterious space;
Bright ruby forms bathing in clouds of pearl,
Resting so gracefully in golden world.

How nature lavishly bestows her gifts—
But list!
Who comes to break upon my revery?

[*Enter* EUPHEMIA.]

What is so wonderful,
Grim prophetess?

EUPHEMIA.

Oh, wonderful indeed!
Most wonderful!

JOSEPHINE.

Bad fortune is't, or good?

EUPHEMIA.

Ah who can tell what's good or bad for us ?
Your hand bodes evil, but your face, your face
As plainly speaks of happiness—yes, great
And lofty happiness !

JOSEPHINE.

How cautious !
'Tis best when one seeks not to be entrapped,
Yet some great story, wonderful, would tell,
Having but little semblance of the truth ;
But proceed grave oracle !

EUPHEMIA.

I dare not
Speak to you more plainly !   Oh, pardon me !
Let me leave you !

JOSEPHINE.

Stay !   I command you.   Speak !
You shall tell on if good or bad it be !
You go not from my presence till I hear
This strange hallucination through and through.

EUPHEMIA.

Well, since you order it, I must obey—
I must obey !—Your countenance does tell
That destiny has sealed for you a fate

Which, struggle though you may, cannot be
    changed!
Soon you will wed. And ah! alas! how soon
Again husbandless! And then—

JOSEPHINE.

Then! What then?

EUPHEMIA.

You shall be queen of France! Yes, more than
    queen!
And then, glorious life! happiest days
Shall bless you! A mighty emperor shall share
With you his crown.—But ah! alas! alas!
Misfortune then will come!—yet, fondly loved,
A world shall mourn your fall.

                    [Rushes away.

JOSEPHINE, *(laughing)*.

Good bye! good bye! poor old Euphemia!
Seek one who kneels at superstition's shrine,
If thou wouldst win a name for prophecy.

       [Goes to hammock and reclines in it.

"Fate—queen of France—yes, more than queen!
And then glorious life! happiest days
Shall bless you!—A mighty emperor shall share
With you his crown.—But ah! alas! alas!
Misfortune then"—No! I'll not believe it.

Why do I thus permit my silly tongue
To prattle o'er this idle prophecy?

Enter MARY.
I am too happy, seeing you, my love!
Take my guitar and sing to me.

[MARY *sings.*

[*Exit* MARY.

JOSEPHINE (*coming down from hammock*).
Where, where am I?—my hammock?—Martinique?
This is not France!—Oh! oh!—The dream! the
dream!

[*Falls.*

Re-enter MARY.

My sister! Josephine! Josephine!

[*Goes to* JOSEPHINE.

JOSEPHINE.

Oh, Mary, such high happiness! And ah!
Such bitter, bitter grief did follow it!

MARY.
Tell me, dear sister! tell me, Josephine!

JOSEPHINE.
You know I have no thought apart from you;

2

That I have ever, ever shared with you
My confidence, my dearest secret thought !
That in my soul I love you as I would
Find love in heaven   But do you forget
That, from my youth, I never could recall
The simplest action of the brain in sleep ?
In dim outline my dreams sometimes return
Like pictures, yet underneath a veil
Of mystery.   But, when I seek to lift
The veil they vanish ! vanish ! and I see
Only th' incorporeal air.

                              [*Excunt.*

    [*A storm is heard approaching in the dis-
        tance.   It grows nearer ; then clouds
        pass over the sea, as seen through the
        bower, followed by lightning and deep
        rolling thunder.*

                              [*Curtain falls.*

NAPOLEON AND JOSEPHINE.

ACT I.

Seventeen years are supposed to have elapsed.

SCENE FIRST.

PARIS.

HEADQUARTERS OF GENERAL-IN-CHIEF BONAPARTE.

OFFICER OF THE GUARD *and* REYNARD (*a Soldier*) *discovered.*

REYNARD.

You 'ave live in La Corsica? You know ze General?

OFFICER.

The fellow speaks English—   [*aside.*
Yes, have known him from childhood—was with him at Brienne.

REYNARD.

Ze school of ze militaire?

OFFICER.

He remained there until he was sixteen years
of age. .He was always a mystery to us—

REYNARD.

Ah, ha!

OFFICER.

and kept himself apart from us, wearing a sombre
visage—

REYNARD.

Ze look mysterieux!

OFFICER.

and seemed ever wrapped in thought. I have
known him to walk for hours with folded arms
and head bent low, oblivious to all about him.

REYNARD.

He vas look in ze futuaire, ze great futuaire of
La Belle France!

OFFICER.

He lived almost wholly to himself, his books and
his thoughts; but, with a quiet dignity, he ever
bore courteous demeanor, and his friendship was
sought by all. The champion of the cause of the

feeble and oppressed, he had no sympathy with petty tyranny, and ruled us all with a grave authority that we obeyed, not knowing why.

REYNARD.

Ah, ha! Zat is ze qualite militaire! He will be vun great General.

OFFICER.

To me he 'was ever frank, and I became acquainted with many strange and mysterious theories through him ; one of which was a divination from numerical formula.

REYNARD.

Ze look in ze futuaire!

OFFICER.

From the mythology of the ancients he had conceived a strange theory of his own, and I think believed in an actual presiding deity who shaped his own particular destiny.

REYNARD.

Ah, ha! He believe in ze gods of ze Greek and ze Roman ?

OFFICER.

Not altogether as the Greeks and the Romans

believed in them, but in the separate forces they represented.

REYNARD.

Sooblime conceptione!

OFFICER.

But upon these subjects he was very reticent.

REYNARD.

'Ave not mooche to speak—ze great man 'ave not mooche to speak—he 'ave ze t'ought—ze conceptione magnifique! ze graand idea! ze look in ze futuaire.

OFFICER.

I was with him at Toulon, and often near him, for he mixed with us where the fight was hottest, cheering and directing our movements. Once, when the shells flew thick above us, a cannon-ball took off the head of an artillery man, as he was in the act of applying the match. The General stooped, and taking the match from the dead man's hand, discharged the gun, and then, for several hours, kept his post with the rest of us.

REYNARD.

Proud *empressment!* He 'ave ze graand cour-

age! Ah, monsieur, he 'ave ze graand courage!
Ah, ha! you 'ave remembaire ze Thirteenth Vendemiaire? Ah, mon Dieu! ze scream of ze vim-
men! ze shout of ze soldiare! ze moan of ze dying!
ze streets run vis ze blood! ze cannon roar like ze
deep tundiare! Ze balls viz, phew! round ze 'ead
of ze General! He valk in ze blood! He 'ave no
change in ze face—ze look impassione! But he 'ave
ze fire in ze eye! Ah, ha! he 'ave ze fire in
ze eye!

OFFICER.

'T was this success that made him General.

REYNARD.

Vun graand *jour* for *La Belle France* to make
him General!

OFFICER.

I should have been glad to witness the scene
when he rushed into the convention, and, by his
eloquence, turned the tide of affairs.

REYNARD.

I vas on ze guard, I see and 'ear it all. Zat vas
vun graand *jour*, long to be remembaire. Ze conventione 'ave no 'ead, no *queue;* ze membaire all
speak at vun time—" Ze Sections 'ave ze *victoir!*

Ze Sections 'ave ze *victoir !* " come ze vord all ze
vile. Zen come ze armistice from General Menou!
Hell Sacrement! ze confusione, ze uproar! Ze
President, Barras, lose all control. Ah ha! *voila!*
Ze young man viz ze pale face! He rush in ze
conventione! He stop to catch ze bress, and look
vis ze fire eye—zen he make vun graand speech!
Ah mon Dieu! Ze passione, ze eloquence! He
say ze conventione mus not lose vun leetle moment.
I no can remembaire ze grand speech, but he make
vun ver' graand speech! Zen ze conventione give
ze command to ze young man viz ze pale face—ze
command of ze soldaire. Ah, mon Dieu! Zat vas
vun graand *jour* for *La Belle France.*

OFFICER.

But see, he comes! Let us withdraw.

[Exeunt.

Enter BONAPARTE.

BONAPARTE.

'Tis said that when these eyes first saw the light,
They gazed upon a piece of tapestry,
Whereon were painted Iliad's tragic scenes.
And that my father on the bed of death
Recurring to this circumstance of birth,
Made honorable mention of my name,

And said, "Napoleon's sword shall one day rule
And triumph o'er all Europe's haughty pride!"
—How has this thought coursed ever through my
   brain!
Dear childhood! glorious youth! what memories
Linger now with you! What wondrous visions
Hover over you, of future greatness
And immortal fame! How, adown the years,
The one great thought of *power* reigned supreme!
How do the boundless resources of soul,
Armed with this thought, cry Onward! ever on!
Why should I doubt its inspiration's source,
When in my dreams it rings out as a voice
Forth from the lips of the great goddess Fate?
—Odd years do intervene
Between her visits on my natal hour,
Yet each recurring year adds one more star
Unto the crown she holds above my head.
—Seven and three, twice three, and seven, and
   three—
The divination of a unity!
I'll doubt no more!
Jacta est Alea!
—Thou supreme goddess Fate, my mother, hail!
Lo! let the firm alliance now be sealed!
Lead on! lead on!
About it now, good brain,
Thou never-resting! We are dauntless now!

Conceive, and She shall help to execute,
The Indomitable Will !

> [*A noise of quarreling and strife without.*

Enter SOLDIER OF THE GUARD.

SOLDIER.

General, a youth in hot impatience
Waits without, demanding quick admission.

BONAPARTE.

Demanding ?   Well, his name !

SOLDIER.

Eugene de Beauharnais.

BONAPARTE.

Admit him !   Stay ! Let him be attended !

> [*Exit* SOLDIER.

Enter EUGENE, (*attended.*)

BONAPARTE.

Your business must be urgent, Sir, indeed,
Since you do knock so loudly for admission.

EUGENE.

Urgent indeed, thou vicegerent of death !

For at the hands of this base government
We have received such wrongs as loudly call
For honest reparation or revenge!
And at the bar of God will louder call,
For, pay as best you can, you cannot pay
The price that He puts on a single soul.
My mother claims a husband at your hands;
She has a son and daughter who both claim
A father, murdered by your damned decree!
Oh, hell, ope wide your jaws and swallow up
The hideous monsters who now prey on France!

BONAPARTE.

Dare you say the Republic *murdered* your father?

EUGENE.

Aye! More I dare! For what now can I lose?
Thousands of the noblest and best blood
That e'er gave strength to France, were, by this same
Republic which you serve, untimely sent
To moulder in their graves! The very earth
Grew sick, being so forced to overfeed
On human carcasses. But I came not
To plead for France, or for my father who
Now rests, thank God! beyond your wicked pow'r!
I claim my father's sword which recently
Your soldiers forced away. For it was mine,

And on it I have sworn to be like him
Who nobly bore it in his country's cause.
My mother bade me take that oath
And I will keep it sacred while I live.

BONAPARTE.

You seem right noble ; what have you to plead
Why the great mandates of your country should,
In your case more than others, be ignored?

EUGENE.

That which should be a nation's gratitude
To one who ever valiantly did fight
On many bloody, hard contested fields
In her defense, and who at last was slain,
To appease the wrath of her most deadly
And inveterate enemies !
That just right of protection which belongs
To those who are the widows, daughters, sons
Of the defenders of their country's cause
Why, sir, the spirit of true chivalry
Robs not the dead nor strikes a fallen foe,
But to his widow and his orphans gives
As strong an arm as to his own dear rights.
Why gave you up my father's property,
And held it not as lawful confiscate
If that he was a traitor, worthy death ?
And now you take his sword !

What greater right to it than to his lands?
What value is to you this sword?
On whom would you presume to buckle it?
Not in the confines of the Republic
Could be found one who would be worthy of it.

BONAPARTE.

But should I give it you, will you consent
To take an oath that you will wear it
Only in your country's cause?

EUGENE.

A double oath?
If one were virtueless, what greater power
Would bind me in the second? Said I not
That on my father's sword, before high heaven,
I promised to my mother I would be
Like him? And who will dare to say that he,
My noble father, was a traitor?
Or think you that an oath would record find
In heaven given to you, and one before
My mother be refused.

BONAPARTE.

Your mother is,
No doubt, a virtuous, good old lady.

EUGENE.

My mother is both virtuous and good—
Too good, too good and pure that from her eyes
Heartless and wicked men should cause to flow
Such very floods of tears.

BONAPARTE.

Have you no fear,
That with such bold vehemence you upbraid
The rulers of Great France!

EUGENE.

I had just returned
From St. Germain; and when I saw
A vacant place upon the wall where once
Did hang my father's sword, and too was told
How in base mockery and sacrilege
It had thence been ta'en—
And when my mother's weeping eyes, blanched
     cheeks
And trembling form confronted me, I rushed
Out in the street and swore I'd have that sword
Or die in fighting for it!

BONAPARTE.

Come to my arms, thou noble, noble youth!
Happy mother, what else so e'er betide
Whom gracious Heaven has blessed with such a
     son!

Happy the land that claims thee for her own !
Now thou shalt have thy father's sword —
Bring forth Beauharnais' sword !

> [*Exit soldier, who returns with sword.*]

                                 It shall be thine !
There, I will buckle it upon thy thigh.
Now go, and bless thy mother with the sight
Of a most noble and most worthy son !

EUGENE (*kissing sword*).

Oh, General, 'tis well sometimes to lose,
Else should we know how sweet it is to find.

> [*Exit, attended.*]

Ah ! 'tis too true !
Too true the story of this noble youth !
France has passed through that unnatural fire
Which well nigh has consumed her gold and left
But miserable dross.
She had drained the intoxicating cup
Of liberty, and it had made her mad.   ·
But the royal blood of her own children,
Of which she drank so freely, at last cooled
Her burning mania.

> [*Exit.*

Re-enter OFFICER *and* REYNARD.

REYNARD.

    Bravo ! bravo for ze young man !   By gar, he is
vun brave Frenchman.

OFFICER.

He is a noble fellow! I knew his father.

REYNARD.

He is vun brave young man! He 'ave ze grand courage. By gar! I loafe ze young man. He vill make vun brave soldiaire.

OFFICER.

A mother may well be proud of such a son. Have you seen her?

REYNARD.

La Viscountess de Beauharnais? S'e 'ave ze beauty of Martinique, ze grace and polish of France. S'e 'ave ze divine perfectione! Ah, Mon Dieu, ze voice! S'e 'ave ze voice of ze Æolian! You 'ave 'ear no sweet music till you 'ave 'ear zat voice!

OFFICER.

You grow eloquent in her praise.

REYNARD.

Ven you 'ave seen la Belle Dame de la Belle France. Ah ha! you 'ave ze eloquence.

OFFICER.

She must have wedded young to be the mother of so old a son, and yet retain such wondrous beauty.

REYNARD.

You 'ave ze right, but ze young man is not so old as he look.

OFFICER.

Why do you speak English ?

REYNARD.

Ze General 'ave tell me I mus' mastaire ze language.   I mus' obey my General.

Re-enter BONAPARTE.

BONAPARTE.

To REYNARD.]
This to the Directory.   [*Giving dispatch.*

[*Exeunt* OFFICER *and* REYNARD.

Carnot is true as steel !—I like not Barras,
Nor will I trust him.
That man, whose greatest satisfaction
Is persecution and severity
To enemies, can have no friend so dear
But who, if not subservient to him
In his basest ends, he 'll sacrifice.
Though he your shoe may buckle day by day,

3

'T is only that you wear it out for him.
Barras befriends me,
Since I did help him on to his renown,
But let my service cease—farewell Barras !
Carnot is noble, and to him I go
For my commission into Italy.
Give me sweet fame, sweet fame, O Italy !
And I will bury deep the memories
Of the Thirteenth Vendemiaire.

Enter a SOLDIER.

SOLDIER.

The Viscountess de Beauharnais requests an audience.

BONAPARTE.

Admit her.

[*Enter* JOSEPHINE.]

At your service, Madame.

JOSEPHINE.

General Bonaparte :
I come to pay that tribute which belongs
To him who saw more touching eloquence
In youthful words and face than soldiers saw
In woman's tears.　And in the name of him
Who once so honorably bore the sword

Which you have generously returned to us,
His widow and his children, I thank you !
And, if the vehemence and fire of youth
Suggested bitter words in our Eugene,
Accept our deep regret and pardon him !

BONAPARTE.

Viscountess de Beauharnais :
Too well I know the justice of the cause
For which he spoke to censure him.   Rather
Would I praise his noble heroism.
Through wreck of empire and the clouds of war
How few are left of all the pride of France !

JOSEPHINE.

How few—how few.   Yet truth undisciplined
To gentle words, urged on by outraged justice
And impetuous youth, though it be truth,
May give offense, stepping beyond the bounds
Of that true courtesy which indeed belongs
Even to passion.   I can hardly hope
But that Eugene spoke hastily, and owes
A just apology, the which would I
Now pay for him.

BONAPARTE.

Too proud am I for France,
In that she should have left to her a son

Who dares plead eloquently for the right
Against a fearful odds, not counting costs.
Apologies from Eugene! Rather say
From France.

JOSEPHINE.

Accused he not *you*, General,
Being in power?

BONAPARTE.

              The military
Is but the automaton of nations.
The soldier only knows obedience,
Though it should lead him to the cannon's mouth.
Eugene did know this, and his charges laid
With words well seasoned at the proper door,
For which most truly do I honor him;
And, by your gracious leave and his consent,
Would help him to preferments whence he may
Have opportunity to prove to France
And all the world, a true nobility
And lofty genius.

JOSEPHINE.

          I thank you—thank you!
Ah, Sir, I had despaired of France! Poor France!
Oh, save our country, and in tribute we
Your subjects will forever, ever bless you!
                    [*Offers to go.*

BONAPARTE.

Stay! One moment, pardon me!
Madam, give me but leave to be your guest,
And though in France you find but little hope,
You may an honorable frienship find
In her General.

JOSEPHINE.

For such distinguished honor
I should only be too grateful.

[Offers to go.

BONAPARTE.

One moment more! You are unattended—
My guard awaits your service.

JOSEPHINE.

I thank you!
But, General, you forget my schooling.
The woman who could pass through Robespierre's
     reign,
Has little of that feeling now called fear,
Still less with Bonaparte chief General.

[Exit.

BONAPARTE.

It cannot be a dream!
Of such perfection, dream could ne'er conceive!
—Nay, I am sensible to feeling, touch,
Sight, sound—it is, it is reality!
I breathe—my heart beats—God! 'twill leap from
    me!
—Oh, insignificant and pallid orb,
What lonely twilight's left since she has gone!
Now will I have thee, though it cost all France!
All France!
Oh, beggar's gift! Crowns, scepter, power
Will I add to it — aye, till all the world
Shall do thee homage!
Lands, rivers and great oceans, vieing each
Shall yield their choicest gems to deck thy
    crown,
And fairest climes their flowers, whence gentle
    dews,
Quick'd i' the roseate light shall rise for thee,
In spray of rare perfume, divinely sweet!
On earth an universal happiness,
For thou shalt be the Queen!
—Oh insufficiency!
Thou shouldst have heaven! a coronet of stars!

—If, in the Directory
Good Carnot should succeed—I *must* have France,
And Italy shall lead me to the throne.
France mine, and I have won the stepping-stone
To universal empire.—Now, Glory
Clasps hands with Love, and Fate, supreme o'er
    all,
Points forward!

[*Exit.*

SCENE SECOND.

THE DIRECTORY.

CARNOT, BARRAS, LAREVILLIERE LEPEAUX, REWBELL *and*
LETOURNEUR;—REWBELL *presiding.*

REWBELL.

Citizen Directors :
Again have we assembled in the name
And by the vested power of the Republic.
Let only wisdom's counsels here prevail,
That all the land may safety see in us;
That tenderly we nurse our infant state
Through all the episodes of growing strength—
Happy childhood, ambitious youth, e'en to
A full-grown noble manhood.
We are but yet a bold experiment
Which oft before has wrought a sad defeat ;
Let not our children write upon our tombs :
These were the fathers who but vainly sought
To give to the Republic longer life.
But, to forego a formal opening speech,
Consuming time which is so precious now,
'T is well we fall to work.
Citizen Director Carnot,
Have you report to make touching the strength
And disposition of our armies?
We are in waiting for it, if so be.

CARNOT.

Citizen, President, and Directors :
As last reported, all goes slowly on.
'Tis well, I think, that we do quickly make
Some changes in our officers, and add
New lives to our wasting armies.
I need not trace the detailed history ,
Of that unfruitful, indecisive war
Which for the last four years France has main-
    tained
Against the Austrian and Sardinian arms—
Too well is known to all of you our loss,
Too palpable our national disgrace.
Year by year, we have barely met the foe,
On narrow battle-fields, mid deep defiles
Of towering Alps, and neath the craggy feet
Of the Ligurian Appenines—met,
But not vanquished—only exchanged our blows
For blows which we received.   Till now,
An army weak, and miserably clad,
Without provisions wholesome e'en for brutes,
Relaxed in discipline, ambitionless,
Cursing their country, and no less themselves
For its neglect, their own torpidity ;
Five-and-thirty thousand of such men as these,
And an imbecile for General,
Are all that now is left to us of what
Was once a noble army of brave men.

Look around you!   What have we to meet?
England, Austria, Bavaria, Piedmont,
Naples, and some minor States of Germany
And Italy—all joined to Austria's league.
The key is Italy,
Held by the army of Beaulieu,
Full sixty thousand brave, well-marshaled men.
What follows?
Shall we retain as General, Scherer,
Because there is no bold apparent crime
On which to bring an accusation ?
What greater crime can generals commit
Than failure?
No less we need, Directors,
Than one who can at once inspire with life
And a new courage give our broken troops,
With *genius* to command and marshal them
To victory!
E'en such an one have we
In Toulon's conqueror, our once defender,
Now our General, Napoleon Bonaparte.
   With all due courtesy to others' views,
I do a step most firmly advocate
Deposing General Scherer, and his place
Give o'er to Bonaparte.

LEPEAUX.

Citizen Directors:
Let us guard well, lest those may be deposed

Whom circumstances have combined against,
And, though possessing ample skill at arms,
Have made short progress.

BARRAS.

Citizen, President, and worthy colleagues:
The very force and weight of argument
Of worthy Citizen Carnot, must be
To all apparent.   France long has been disgraced
By sad mismanagement in Italy.
'T is well we look to it.
Now press on every hand the combined force
Of Austria and her firm allies.
To right, to left, without, within, around,
And everywhere the foes of France are thick!
Sleeping or waking, we are beset with spies,
Our councils filled with foul distempered knaves,
Our people, by old feuds held separate,
Sowing germs of discord quick'd i' the sun
At every noon.
Who knows but by to-morrow's dawn
We shall find safety only in defense
Or flight from some self-constituted power,
Like that of the Thirteenth Vendemiaire?
We stand too long fearing lest we offend!
The times demand quick action—let 's amend!
The key of Austria's strength is Italy!
The key of our success is Italy!

Then let us strike the foe in Italy !
First bring we home this Scherer, long worn out,
A rank offense to France and to our arms ;
Supplant him with our Bonaparte, and give
" Achilles " a fair field for enterprise.
Then shall proud Austria and her allies feel
What 't is to meet the great Republic's steel !

LETOURNEUR.

Citizen Directors :
Do we forget our hero 's but a youth
Compared to those whose fame is no less great,
Who have grown gray in honorable service?
The Corsican, in truth, deserves great praise,
But is not Italy too heavy weight
For strength so tender !   Why look you, I pray,
He is scarce twenty-five—

CARNOT.

Aye ! almost as young, good Letourneur,
As Alexander ! Scipio ! or Conde !
Why, worthy sir, our Bonaparte has lived
A quarter of a century !

REWBELL, *Pres.*

Citizen Directors :
Our subject is too weighty for great haste,
I pray you now at once give o'er debate

Until we next convene.   Meanwhile reflect
As well becomes the step we are to take.

> [*Exeunt all but* BARRAS.

BARRAS.

Yes, yes! for young "Achilles" the best place
Is Italy!
He grows too fast—I'll nip him in good time
Ere this green fruitage of his glory
Shall ripen into power.
Now, then, "Achilles," ho! for Italy!
Oh, dear Beaulieu, Barras sends, greeting thee,
Petit "Achilles."

> [*Exit.

REYNARD. (*Coming from concealment.*)
Ah! ha! Monsieur Barras; Reynard, ze fox,
vill make zis graand speech to ze General.   By
Gar, I vas like to *pique* you vis my rappier!

> [*Exit.

SCENE THIRD.

Drawing-room of Viscountess de BEAUHARNAIS. JOSE-
PHINE, AUGUSTA *and* BARRAS, *with number of Ladies
and Gentlemen, in conversation* BONAPARTE *off to
himself.*
[*Exit all but* BONAPARTE *and* JOSEPHENE.

BONAPARTE.

Your pardon, Madam!
'Twas not through want of due respect that I
Was so oblivious—
Your chart of Italy is most correct,
Though small, as I have learned of it;
When overwhelmed in thought it is my fault
That I, oftimes, neglect the courtesy
That rightfully is due to—

JOSEPHINE.

You certainly are quite excusable!
For, in these days, those who protect our land
Have little time for social intercourse.

BONAPARTE.

Most true—most true—
And yet the object of my visit here
Is of a nature least akin to war—
I am in love.

JOSEPHINE.

Not always least akin to war,
Good General, but very often brings
Its victims least of peace. Yet, may I know,
Since you already volunteer so much,
The name of her so honored with the love
Of Toulons' conqueror, the General of France?

BONAPARTE.

With all my heart, as all my heart is yours!
I love you! Be my wife!

JOSEPHINE.

                 Is it a jest
You would indulge?

BONAPARTE.

              Look I as one who jests?
My life has been
As restless ever as a storm-tossed sea,
Seeking something it could not find,
Seeking it knew not what, yet feeling
As if it were no more than half itself.
I said, 'It is ambition,' sought for fame,
And easily obtained it; yet a thirst
Burning and torturing me was unquenched.
Above the clang
Of clashing steel, the din of frightful war,

Still came a soul-cry yet unsatisfied,
When, like an angel spirit all unbid,
Thou didst appear, dear empress of my soul!
—In silence looks the Supreme Goddess down,
Still beckoning me on to other fields.
Lo! in defiance of all power above,
Beneath, I claim your hand, and at your feet
Will prostrate all! aye, even to a world!

JOSEPHINE.

Marriage
Is fraught with consequence but less than death!
One for this life seals a fate, the other
For that longer life which is to come.

BONAPARTE.

Though well assured of this, still do I urge
My suit.

JOSEPHINE.

          But have you well considered all,
My age, my children and my former love?

BONAPARTE.

All this and more, and more.

JOSEPHINE.

          What more?

BONAPARTE.

Myself.

JOSEPHINE.

I do not understand.

BONAPARTE.

My *love* is all
That I can offer in exchange for these—
But oh, that love is life, soul, all! my heaven!
—Speak! Is't or life or death?

JOSEPHINE.

Oh do not think my life currents run cold!—
Experience makes us considerate.

BONAPARTE.

The future, the fair future is before us;
Life will date anew from that bright moment
We are one. Love is an eternal springtime!

JOSEPHINE.

Nay, do not pause, speak on! Your words do
  thrill
With that strange ecstacy of which I've dreamed
Though never felt till now—
Ah! Ah! that fate should stand between us!

4

BONAPARTE.

Fate!
Can it be that Fate appears to her?   (*aside.*)

JOSEPHINE.

It seems stern fate forbids that I should be
The wife of General Bonaparte.

BONAPARTE.

Madam, do you seek to trifle with me?

JOSEPHINE.

No! No! I am indeed most serious!
I cannot be your wife since I am destined
To be Queen of France.

BONAPARTE.

Pray you, explain!

JOSEPHINE.

In Martinique a prophetess foretold
My fortune.   So far, her words oracular
Have been fulfilled; conclude I, then, the rest
Will yet be realized.

BONAPARTE.

Give me her words!

JOSEPHINE.

" You shall be Queen of France.   Yes, more than
    Queen !
And then, glorious life ! happiest days
Shall bless you !   A mighty Emperor shall share
With you his crown !
But ah ! alas ! misfortune then will come !
Yet, fondly loved, a world shall mourn your fall.'

BONAPARTE.

To Fate I bid defiance !   Be my wife !

JOSEPHINE.

Your wife—your wife—

BONAPARTE.

Aye, my wife !
You muse right strangely.   Gather the clouds
So darkly in the morning sky of love ?

JOSEPHINE.

Nay !   It seems the rose-tint deepens
As I gaze upon the rising beams of light !
And now it melts into the white !   And now
A flood of glory bathes the world !
Oh is it now the morning of my life ?
The night was long and dark, so dark !

BONAPARTE.

No night
Less glorious than the day, with such a star
As thou to hallow it!

JOSEPHINE.

Art thou the Sun
That lifts the sable curtains of my night?
Oh world! Thou art too small for this hour's
ecstacy!

BONAPARTE.

Oh come, and we will rise even beyond
This hour! Aye, even to companionship
Of gods!

JOSEPHINE.

Ah, let me lean upon thee first;
Yet am I weak, and tremble 'neath my load
Of joy! When I am stronger I will learn
To bear my rapture.

BONAPARTE.

Thou *shalt* be queen of France! and reign,
As now, most absolute o'er my fond soul!
Fair Empress, e'er your hand the scepter bear,
Let it receive, in token of fealty,
A kiss most sacred since it is my first.

Enter a PAGE.

PAGE.

Le Monsieur Ragideau.

JOSEPHINE.

To Bonaparte.]
'T is some affair of business, I think.

BONAPARTE.

Give him audience; I will retire.

[*Retires to recess in drawing-room.*

JOSEPHINE.

Admit Monsieur Ragideau !

[*Exit* PAGE.

Enter RAGIDEAU.

RAGIDEAU.

There is a private matter, not indeed
So much of business as interwoven
With your prosperity and happiness.
And, with deference to your prerogative,
I should be found unworthy of your trust
As honorable Advocate, should I
Not warn you of so hazardous a step

As that you contemplate in second marriage.
Your friends have looked with much alarm
Upon this change, fraught with so great hazard.

JOSEPHINE.

Our affairs, it seems, are known by others
Ere they come to us.   (*aside*).
                    But my dear Advocate
Do you share with my friends in this alarm ?

RAGIDEAU.

Madam, you are rich and independent ;
Five-and-twenty thousand francs is no mean sum
To come in yearly—too much to give away.
You are young, beautiful ! yes, beautiful !
I am no flatterer, madam, that you know ;
I am your Advocate, and I tell you,
You can command who e'er you will.
General Bonaparte may be noble,
Good, generous, brave—he is a soldier,
And poor—he must abide the fate of war ;
He must be separate from you—live so,
For 'tis a soldier's lot—*Fame* is not sure.
There are few Cæsars, Alexanders few,
Yet millions have their graves untimely found,
Seeking that which few do gain.
Put each of you the same at stake, Madame,
The case would then be very different ;

But in the scale, all else being equal,
Your purse would quite outweigh his sword and
    hat.

JOSEPHINE.

But he is honorable, brave and true!
Worships me as his idol!—Have I not
A purse that's strong enough for both?

RAGIDEAU.

Let me suppose a case:—You marry;—
Another revolution overthrows
Our government;—General Bonaparte
Is conspicuous in the Republic;—
His property and yours are confiscate,
And you are left to do the best you can—
Perhaps to suffer. I have not overdrawn;
History proves the instability
Of new—yes, all—republics. Besides,
Ever harrassed with fear, the soldier's wife
Knows not whether she be wife or widow.

JOSEPHINE *(laughing).*

What think you, General? what think you now
Of my good Advocate's advice?

                    [BONAPARTE *comes*
    forward and takes RAGIDEAU *by the hand.*

BONAPARTE.

Monsieur Ragideau has spoken honestly!
I can but honor him the more for it.
I trust his fears may not be realized,
And that he will to us give his consent,
His office to continue.   Such a man
May well be trusted.

[*Exeunt.*

[*Enter from one side* AUGUSTA *and* HOR-
TENSE; *from the other,* EUGENE.

EUGENE.

I am glad to meet you.

HORTENSE.

We to meet you.
But brother, you surprise us!

EUGENE.

It seems I am
Required to-night at the headquarters
Of General Bonaparte.

HORTENSE.

Do you know
The cause for which he summons you?

EUGENE.

Well, no!
And yet I do surmise it is to make
A soldier of me.

AUGUSTA *and* HORTENSE.

A soldier?

AUGUSTA.

No! no!

EUGENE.

From what he did convey as his intent
To my mother and myself, I must think
This is his purpose.

HORTENSE.

But you will not go?
[EUGENE *crosses to* AUGUSTA.
There's something deeper, then, than sister's love?
[*Exit.*

EUGENE.

Nay, sweetheart, sweetheart, do not be so sad!

AUGUSTA.

And will you go even though it is his wish?

EUGENE.

My will is yours, I have no other, Sweet,

Save when you will less for yourself than me.
The General's wish is near akin to law—
Yet it may be that I am wrong in what
I have inferred.   And still, if I be right,
Let it not rest so heavy on your heart!
We must remember, Love—nay ne'er forget—
That sorrow, hardly less than that which now
Does threaten us, did bring me to your side.

AUGUSTA.

Oh, would you leave me for the phantom Fame?

EUGENE.

Leave you? No!   No! Nay, not for all the world,
Though it should lie an off'ring at my feet.
Ah, without you, how empty it would be!
Augusta, I cannot conceive of heaven
Without you.

AUGUSTA.

Eugene!   Eugene!

EUGENE.

                                    Augusta,
Hear me! oh for a voice to tell my love!—
Impossible!   On such a theme all words
Are impotent.   Not long ago I stood
Beside the sea; a distant storm had lashed

The waves into a furious mutiny,
Until they rolled high up upon the beach,
A mountain range of spray, sun-kissed to pearls !
Oh, 't was sublimely beautiful ! and yet
It had but little charm for me, dear love !
—But yesterday I visited the scenes
Of Fontainbleau—its forests and chateau,
Where man and nature join their highest art—
And as, from scene to scene, my eyes did pass
Where other eyes do find such fair delight,
A longing, then as now unutterable,
Filled my breast for you, and all comfortless
I turned away to drink the zephyrs
Wafted from your home.
I measure all, weigh all, count all by you !
The height of heaven is measured by your love !
The weight of worlds my love for you outweighs !
And every moment counts as nothing,
Or with you !

AUGUSTA.

Eugene, I know you love me !
And oh, do you remember that fair dream
When, sitting on the border of a stream,
I watched the swans gliding o'er sunlit waves,
The fragrant breath of water-lilies
Lingering with song of birds upon the air ?
The while I thought of you, and wished that you

Were by my side?   And how a little boat
Turned round the stream's quick curve ere I had
        wished?
You sprang from it to clasp me in your arms
And press your loving lips to mine—
Until at last the hour sped, I waked
In parting from you.   Let me tell you now
What followed this a few weeks afterward.
—Not far from where I dreamed there is a lake
Within the borders of a lonely park;
And flowing into it there is a stream,
Not unlike that my dream disclosed to me.
And this I visited some two months since;
The swans were at my feet, and lilies sweet,
And songs of birds, all just as I had seen
Them in my dream, were now reality.
I lifted up my eyes to look for you—
An empty, empty boat came round the bend!
The agony of that one moment was
An hundred deaths!   Eugene, thou wilt not go?

EUGENE.

This was some two months past, yet have we seen
Many sweet hours together since that time.
If this strange circumstance have meaning, 'tis
That, my short absence o'er, I will return
To find with you new joys, as we have had
Since then.   Good cheer! Good cheer! I may not go,

Yet if I do 'twill be but to return
And lay my honors at your feet.

AUGUSTA.

For your absence what *honors* could repay?
Think you I care for honors? Oh my love!
I would not have you greater than you are—
Great as the world calls great; to me there is
Nothing so high but that you are above,
Beyond it! Nay, I could not wish for aught
I do not find in you. What could I add
Unto your excellence? Eugene! Eugene!

EUGENE.

Would you not see me honored among men,
Commanding armies, wielding sword and pen
Until my fame should reach throughout the world?

AUGUSTA.

Those whom men honor are of little worth.
God honors who are nearest like Himself.
For one who rises many sure must fall.
I would not see your greatness builded
On broken hearts and desolated homes,
And though your fame should run throughout the
        world,
I could not love you more than I do now.
I am content with you just as you are,
And would not have you one jot different.

EUGENE.   \

My dear Augusta! would that I could feel
That I were worthy of such love as this;
Though 'twas with pride I heard the General speak,
I only saw my future as for you.
Achievement else were hollow mockery.
—But come! you shall know all without delay.
Good bye!   Good bye!

[Offers to go.

AUGUSTA.

Eugene, when on the field of battle, will you ask
Yourself, ere you decide to take a step
Wherein great danger lies,
" What would Augusta have me do?"   And I
Will ever ask, even in lightest matters,
" What would my Eugene counsel?" Must you go?
I cannot, cannot give you up, Eugene!
There are a thousand things that I would say!
I cannot let you go!—Farewell.

[Exit EUGENE.

Eugene!   Eugene!   (*falls.*)

[Scene Changes to a Tableau; BONAPARTE, *Mounted,
Leading the Armies of France.*]

[Curtain falls.

END OF ACT I.

ACT II.

SCENE FIRST.

PARLORS OF MADAME BONAPARTE.

BARRAS *discovered.—Enter a* PAGE.

PAGE.

Madame Bonaparte
Regrets she cannot grant you audience
At once, but begs you will remain. Meantime
Permit me to serve you.

[*Exit* PAGE. *Returns with wine. Exit.*

BARRAS.

The musty adage of a "a prophet's fame"
Does not apply, it seems, to one who drinks.
—Wine deadens, is dull-mettled,
Takes hold upon the senses, rocks to sleep ;
A sweet sleep, but it lasts too long by half!
'T is terrible to wake from it!
What have we here ? Ah ! Cognac, by Jove !
Oh, thou sparkling beauty ! queen of my soul !
Thou giv'st an hundred years in one !

[*Drinks.*

Married! and off to Italy!
So soon to quit her!   Oh, most cruel speed!
'T is foulest slander on both sexes, this,
That full-blown manhood could, for such a cause,
Give o'er the very paragon of love!
The perfect pattern—nay, the goddess—
Of pure symmetry!   Ye gods! for fruit so rich
I'd bid the world good-night, and leave to fools
The flimsy glories of uncertain fame.
Were 't mine, this citadel of pleasure,
I'd dwell in it, nor e'er be seen without.
Patriotism!   Bah!
The chameleon dish, well stew'd with fame,
Seasoned all through and through with promises,
Then served with golden spoon of patronage
By those in power, to ambitious fools
Whom they would use.   Barras would prize a throne
For what it added unto his desires;
Nor risk too much obtaining it, since now
His cup's well filled.   For in your graveyard glory
He could never find a relish.
Then live ye for the future those who will!
Barras, in this life, seeks to find his fill.
By Jove! this Bonaparte
Has left rich pasturage for some man's colt!
I'll look to 't!   Who has better right?
I helped him to his greatness, 'tis but just

He should repay me.   I'll prescribe the terms;
My choice of coin!   I'll not take the Republic's,
But that of Royalty, less circulate;
Recently new stamped, but not impaired.
Oh, Beaulieu! trip *"petit* Achilles,"
And leave to me the sighing widow!
—Now to the Directory!
If Bonaparte do meet success, why then
'Twas Barras raised him to his great command!
But if he fall—as fall I pray he may,
Since I do fear this growing Corsican—
Then on poor Carnot's shoulders rests the blame.
And yet, before she comes, a health
To *"petit* Achilles!"   And yet again
To that which he has left his friend!

Enter JOSEPHINE.

I do regret, Monsieur Barras,
To have kept you so long waiting!

BARRAS.

Pardon
The untimely call!   The affairs of State,
In these most busy and eventful times,
Demand us unawares.

JOSEPHINE.

Monsieur, have you
Advice from Italy!

BARRAS.

For this I called—
The General, through his brother and Junot,
Sends this to you; they to no other hands
Would trust it than my own, being themselves
Detained. I came at once to you, and beg,
If any further service I can give, [*Hands a letter.*
You will be pleased the happiness to grant
Of such employment.

JOSEPHINE.

I am most grateful
To you, Monsieur, and if I find a need
Of further favors from such a friendship
I shall be free to acquaint you of it.
[*Exit* BARRAS.

Enter AUGUSTA *and* HORTENSE.

HORTENSE.

Oh mother! more letters?

JOSEPHINE (*reading*).

"My Darling best of Friends :
My brother will hand you this letter. I cherish
for him the most intimate friendship. I trust he
will also gain your affection. He deserves it. Nature has gifted him with a tender and inexhaustibly
good character ; he is full of rare qualities.
I have received your letters of the 21st. You

have indeed for many days forgotten to write to
me. What, then, are you doing? Yes, my friend,
I am not exactly jealous, but I am sometimes un-
easy. Hasten then, for I tell you beforehand if
you delay I shall be sick. So great exertion, combined with your absence, is too much. Your letters
are the joys of my days, and my happy days are
not too many.

Junot takes to Paris twenty-two standards. You
will come back with him, will you not? Misery
without remedy, sorrow without comfort, unmiti-
gated anguish will be my portion, if it is my
misfortune to see him come back alone, my own
adored wife! He will breathe at your shrine, and
perhaps you will even grant him the special and
unsurpassed privilege of kissing your cheek, and I
will be far, far away! You will come here, at my
side, to my heart, in my arms! Take wings, come!
come! Yet journey slowly—the road is long, bad,
fatiguing. If some calamity should happen—if
the exertion—— Set out at once, my beloved one,
but travel slowly.

BONAPARTE."

Will I come to thee? Ask the tender flower
If it will turn its fair face to the sun
For life and strength! or God's sweet choristers
If they will sing in praise to Him who gives
The bright day for their happiness!—
Even as the soul would swiftly take its flight
Unto the source of its supremest ecstasy,
I come! my love, I come!
—How keen the edge of sweet expectancy!

And how it pricks us on to realize
What hope holds up to view!   Yet how often
Do we in possession find less joy
Than in the dreaming of it ere 'twas ours!
"No, no, 'tis not true! this time 'twill not be true."
We say, and yet how seldom does it fail!

AUGUSTA.

Then if, indeed, most happiness exists
In that expectancy which does precede
Reality, let us employ it ere
We cheat ourselves of both.

Enter EUGENE (*in uniform*).

AUGUSTA.

Eugene!   (*falling in his arms.*)

JOSEPHINE.

This is surprise most happy, Eugene!
How long since you left Italy?

EUGENE.

I came
With Joseph Bonaparte, Junot,
And an escort, that did the trophies bring
Of our great victories.   Your letter too.

AUGUSTA.

Eugene!

JOSEPHINE.

How fares the General?

EUGENE.

Did he not

Inform you?

JOSEPHINE.

Oh yes, but tell me, tell me, ,
Is he indeed well? For he ever puts
On everything the best face possible.

EUGENE.

He was in *perfect* health on my departure.
Traces of care do seem to line his face,
Yet these but lend a finer dignity,
If such be possible. Aside from this,
And that he has some stouter grown, he is
As when he quitted France. He bade me add
The fairest words I knew to what he wrote;
And then assure you all was but a tithe
Of that rich tribute he would pay to you
Were words more eloquent.

AUGUSTA.

And spake he not
Of me?

EUGENE.

After remembrance and his love,
He left the rest to me, wherein he said
You would find more delight.   To sweet Hortense,
He sent an hundred kisses and this ring;
The one I give now, and the others will
Before I go.

JOSEPHINE.

So he remembers all!
How rich is he in every tender thought
That lends to manhood the fair lustre
Of love's constancy.

Enter a PAGE.

PAGE.

Madame Therese de Talien.

JOSEPHINE.

Say that I attend her.   Come, Hortense!
                    [*Exit* JOSEPHINE *and* HORTENSE.

AUGUSTA.

How slowly have the hours dragged, Eugene!

Yet I am paid for all a thousand times
In this sweet moment on your breast.

EUGENE.

Have you forgot
How at your feet I used to sit, the while
I told, in fondest words I knew, my love?
And held up fairest pictures of the life
In store for us?   What castles did we build!
What happy visions rose before us then!
But none that equalled this reality.   -
There was one look sweeter than all the rest,
You gave to me at times.   It was a look
You could not give unto another,
For your very soul was couched in it!
There! there!   It beams up to me now!
O my darling!
—How that one look has nestled in my heart
Through all the weary hours of absence!
How has it cheered me when all else was vain!
How, like a light from heaven let down to me,
Illumed my path, and as a beacon
Brought me back to you!

AUGUSTA.

Speak on, that I may hear the music
Of your voice!   It has been long, so long,
Since I have listened to it, Love!   Speak on!

I love your praise, not for the praise, but that
It tells me of your love!   Speak on!

EUGENE.

Your very beauty robs me of my words!
What eloquence could rise to such a theme !
Yet, since it may delight you, I will tell
Of a most lovely scene of which I dreamed
On yesternight—
A sunlit vale
Where perfumed grasses were all interspersed
With flowers rare and rich—sweet mignonette,
And heliotrope, innumerable
Roses, and nameless flowers as redolent ;
And there were little bowers of jessamine,
Whose balmy breath is but less sweet than that
Wherein your kisses nestle ;—all these did freight
Soft zephyrs, that floated through the glen
And circled round my head in eddying swirl.
There seemed a melody of song to rise
From grass and flower, and the birds caught this
And carried it into the higher measures
Of their dulcet strains!   Then it did echo
Through the glen until, following down
The fringes of the stream that ran just through
The center of the vale, it lost itself
Upon the boundless sea.
Here and there were quiet little nooks

And fair retreats 'neath denser foliage
In every hue and matchless tint of green.
And some old trees, staid warders of the vale,
Were rich with clambering roses,
Or clematis, that graced their massive trunks,
Or other vines luxuriant,
That sought the very topmost boughs to peep
Out first in loveliest blossom and catch
The morning glory of the sun.
Fair clouds
Were ever blushing in divinest tints,
Casting the softest shadows on the vale
Beneath.
    And but one charm was wanting

AUGUSTA.

And that?

EUGENE.

Your presence, darling, then 'twould nothing lack
Of heaven for Eugene.

[*Re-enter* JOSEPHINE.]

JOSEPHINE.

    Some deep design
Is working now against us, something new;
Barras is at the bottom of 't again.

EUGENE.

What have you learned?   'Tis well that I am here.

JOSEPHINE.

Yes, for we'll have a trusty messenger.

EUGENE.

What is't?   Impart!

JOSEPHINE.

A scheme is now on foot,
Laid by the crafty Barras and Gohier;
By which our General is to be betrayed
Into the hands of Beaulieu.   Botot
Is sent a secret messenger to-day
To help dispatch this business.

EUGENE.

Of whom
And by what means is all this known?

JOSEPHINE.

Our friend, Therese de Talien.

EUGENE.

But how
And by what fortune learned she this?

JOSEPHINE.

From him,
Le Monsieur himself, o'er whom she has
An absolute control. For know, he is
At once a pliable and simple fool
In presence of a pretty woman.

EUGENE.

Well, then he can be useful made to us,
More than Barras and the conspirators,
For we have the most witching loveliness
In France.

JOSEPHINE.

A pretty compliment!
But we have little time for such to-day.

EUGENE.

Are others implicated in the plot?

JOSEPHINE.

Only by inference; as he himself
Is not committed in a way that we
Could use as evidence.

EUGENE.

We will mature
Our plans and, by to-morrow, after him.

AUGUSTA.

But why such haste away?   Where go you now?

EUGENE.

It is the hour when the Directory
Will be surprised with what we did bring back
From Italy.   They are in waiting for me.
My duty done, I will return to you.

[*Exeunt.*

SCENE SECOND.

LUXEMBOURG.—THE DIRECTORY.

CARNOT, BARRAS, LAREVILLIERE LEPEAUX, REWBELL,
LETOURNEUR.—SECRETARIES *and* SOLDIERS.—CARNOT
presiding.

Enter a COURTIER.

COURTIER.

General Joseph Bonaparte, Junot and Beauharnais, with tidings from the seat of war in Italy.

CARNOT.

Immediately admit them.

[*Exit* COURTIER.

[*Enter* JOSEPH BONAPARTE, JUNOT, EUGENE,
followed by COURTIERS, *bearing standards.*

JOSEPH BONAPARTE.

Citizen President and Directors :
The General of France sends, greeting you,
Trophies of victory from Italy,
And would most humbly lay them at your feet
As at the shrine of France.

CARNOT.

Sends he report ?
We wait for it most eagerly !

JOSEPH BONAPARTE.

[*Taking banner on
which was inscribed the bulletin.*

He has indeed great victories to tell,
And on our flag inscribes this bulletin :

(*Reads on one side.*) "To the army of Italy,
the grateful country."

(*Reads on other side.*) 115,000 prisoners, 170
standards, 550 pieces of battering cannon, 600
pieces of field artillery, 5 bridge equipages, 9 sixty-
four gun ships, 12 thirty-two gun frigates, 12 cor-
vettes, 18 galleys. Armistice with the King of
Sardinia, Convention with Genoa, Armistice with
the Duke of Parma, Armistice with the King of
Naples, Armistice with the Pope, Preliminaries of
Leoben, Convention of Montebello with the Re-

public of Genoa, Treaty of Peace with the Emperor at Campo Formo, Liberty given to the People
of Bologna, Ferrara, Modena, Massa Carrara, La
Romagna, Lombardy, Bressera, Bornio, The Val-
entina, The Genoese, The Imperial Fiefs, the
People of the Departments of Coreigra, of the
Ægean Sea, and of Ithaca. Sent to Paris all the
masterpieces of Michael Angelo, of Genercino,
of Titian, of Paul Veronese, of Corregio, of Albano
of Carracu, of Raphael and of Leonardo da Vinci.

> *During the reading of this report,* CARNOT
> *is greatly agitated. As the report
> progresses, all rise to their feet.* CAR-
> NOT *comes down from his chair. Tear-
> ing the clothes from his breast, he dis-
> plays a minature of* NAPOLEON, *which
> he had concealed there—holding it up
> to* JOSEPH BONAPARTE.

CARNOT.

Tell your brother
That I do wear him next unto my heart.
>   (*turns to Directors.*)
Go fire your guns! Ring wildly every bell!
Scream with the fife! Let the shrill bugle tell;
With clang of steel, and the unmuffled drum,
And loud huzzas, that victory has come!

Fire, fire the guns!　Let deep-toned thunder roll
Throughout great France, filling each patriot soul
With victory's shouts uprising from the heart,—
Vive la Republic!　Vive le Bonaparte!

ALL (*except* BARRAS).

Vive la Republic!　Vive le Bonaparte!

> *Shouting, cannons, bells and drums without.*
> *Scene changes to Paris, illuminated.*

[*Curtain falls.*

END OF ACT II.

ACT III.

SCENE FIRST.

MILAN.

Drawing-room of the Palace of Serbelloni. BONA-
PARTE *and* EUGENE *discovered reading.*

BONAPARTE.

Contemptible !
That this should be permitted is most strange !
It surely is within the power
Of the Directory to punish this
As for any other treasonable words ;
For *we* are France, no less ! and these attacks,
Against us personally, are no less
Than against our France.

EUGENE.

Their silence proves
The sympathy of the Directory
With your worst enemies from jealousy
Of you.

BONAPARTE.

And yet cannot I understand why they
Should be so blinded to the interests

Of France, nay even their own interests,
Most selfish, as to let this jealousy
Creep in and so despoil them in a night
Of all the vantage they might borrow
From the lustre of my star.   They cannot think
That I will patiently endure this long!
Do they not realize that I have power
To *crush* them, each and all, as with this hand
I crush this evidence of spleen most foul?

                    [*Takes up another journal.*

Here 's language bears the spirit of Barras,
Unless I miss—
These are his words.   Can it be possible
That he should such a peevish bungler be
As to permit peculiar trick of speech
To thus betray him in the public print?—
So—so—I 'll have a closer eye on you,
Monsieur Barras!—I never trusted him,
Eugene, you know I never trusted him.

EUGENE.

And in despising him, I now,
As ever, find a keen delight!

BONAPARTE.

That is unworthy of you, dear Eugene;
Great souls do not descend to it.   Nor this
Nor envy ever dwells within the hearts

6

Of the truly great.—In youth 't is pardoned,
But must be outgrown.—These wasps may sting us,
And the sting may itch—there 's poison in it—
So it may fret the skin, but that is all.

                                        [*Reads.*

" He keeps the plunder "—Rare rhetoricians!
To what do they refer ?—" He does affect
A heartless despotism, overrides
All law "—This is abominable!
To " *affect!* "   To " affect *despotism!* "—
What masterly envenomed slander this!
I like the knave and will requite him for 't.
—I am humiliated when I know
They have the power to annoy me thus.
Eugene, it is these *little* things that fret
And so disturb us, more than all else
In the vicissitudes of life.   Henceforth
Let us look above and far beyond them.
Philosophy,
This, this is the one source of strength, Eugene.
Who lives the butt and sport of daily circumstance,
Is no more than a moth in sunbeam basking,
To drift, before the first vagrant zephyr,
On to the little death that waits him.
But he who can despise, or grief or joy,
With will indomitable, pressing on
Unto the goal of his ambition,
Only wins.

Were 't not that he must eat and sleep, I 'd say
A man might come to be great.

[*Exit.*

Enter JOSEPHINE.

EUGENE.

Mother,
There 's none I may approach but you in this
That weighs so heavy on my heart!   Pardon
And hear me :—For years I have admired,
Nay, loved—nay more—adored, Augusta !
She has the object been of every hope,
Ambition, prayer !   Oh, I have worshiped her!
My highest pleasure was alloyed with pain
Unless she shared it with me.   Greater joys
Were quite impossible ; I could not know
A happiness without her, but *with* her
Was continual ecstasy.   And she,
She loved me, it did seem, even as her life.
"Think of me when you will," she one time wrote,
"Of you I am *ever* thinking, darling,
And loving you, oh very, very dearly!"
Enough!   She loved me then.   But now, no more!

JOSEPHINE.

This confidence I do appreciate—
You have my fullest sympathy, Eugene,
But may I know the cause of all this change ?

EUGENE.

When I know. I have been too fond, I think;
I shrined her goddess in my heart, and she
Would soar now far beyond me. I but pray
That from her airy height she ne'er may fall.

JOSEPHINE.

Eugene!
Why this is madness, boy! Come, tell me all
And I may help you.

EUGENE.

All, all is lost!

JOSEPHINE.

Not all, Eugene. You have your mother left,
And sweet Hortense.

EUGENE.

Ah, yes, I know, I know—
I love you very dearly, but my heart
Did worship her! It knows no heaven beyond.
For you and for Hortense, I'll leave—a name!

JOSEPHINE.

Eugene
Speaks like himself in this. And yet why *leave*

A name? Why not share your honors with us?
You now are in the morning of your life,
And glory seems already hovering close
About your head. You will be great, Eugene,
And good, I trust

EUGENE.

Shall Love step out
And Greatness enter? Farewell to glory
Were easier said than farewell love!
One is of earth, the other infinite!

JOSEPHINE.

But come, you have not yet conveyed to me
The evidence that she is false to you.
You may be rash.

EUGENE.

Rash! Hear me and then judge.
Though near what should have been our wedding-
day,
Berlin has held rare charms for her. Her absence
Bore full heavily upon me, for I,
It seemed, could only think or dream of her—
With *her* how different the sequel-shows.
Though, when she said farewell, she wept
Right bitterly—she *must* have loved me then!
—At first her letters in succession came

As she had promised them. So eloquent,
In sweet simplicity of love, that I
Was lifted into rapture. Followed then
Less frequent, shorter,
Till, from my friends, I learned that she had been
Attended close and constant by Botot.
To-day she did return, a week before
I did expect her, and with this Botot,
Who was still near her but an hour ago—
With me she has not deigned to meet.

JOSEPHINE.

Eugene,
I think that I do understand it all—
Wait my return !

[*Exit* JOSEPHINE.

EUGENE.

She almost bade me hope, when there is no hope!
From such a fall as this we may not rise.
—A brilliant life will, haply, shorter be—
E'en as a falling star, whose light goes out
When its effulgence most attracts our view:
So shall my glory through this little world
Blaze like a meteor in the firmament
And then go out forever ! O farewell !
Farewell, Augusta ! *Now* am I resolved !

Re-enter JOSEPHINE.

This did I find in waiting for you.   [*Gives letter.*

[*Exit* JOSEPHINE.

EUGENE (*reads*).

My Dear Eugene :
    I have just dismissed Monsieur Botot, as I had
no further use for him ; having learned all that
was necessary to assist Mme. Bonaparte in her
plans to save the General from a plot that was to
deliver him in person into the hands of the enemy.
    Inasmuch as I have dismissed Monsieur Botot
rather unceremoniously, since his attentions had
become annoying, he may undertake to avenge
himself upon you, and I thought it best to acquaint
you at once with the situation.   This will somewhat
explain the past few weeks, and my sudden return,
till I can see you.   Do not keep me long in waiting, for, after our separation, and the labor and
excitement consequent upon the undertaking that
has happily terminated well, I am all impatience to
meet you.

AUGUSTA.

EUGENE.

Can you ever forgive me?
    [*Exit.*

Enter OFFICER *and* REYNARD.

REYNARD.

Ah, Mon Dieu ! Zis vat you call loafe, make ze
fool of all.

OFFICER.

Yes, 'tis said the greater man the greater fool becomes when Love ensnares him.

REYNARD.

You know Monsieur Botot?

OFFICER.

No!

REYNARD.

He 'ave ze blonde complexion, ze blue eye, and ze big conceit of ze self—he is ze tool of Barras. I 'ave glad to *pique* him vis my rappier!

OFFICER.

Why is he permitted to go?

REYNARD.

Zat ze place 'ave not vun of more dainjare.

OFFICER.

When do you go to Paris?

REYNARD.

In ze morrow.

OFFICER.

You are a lucky fellow.

REYNARD.

I vill 'ave some dainjare—Barras 'ave great powair, and I am ze spy, ze leetle fox to vatch him.

OFFICER.

To whom do you report?

REYNARD.

Ze General, *la Madame Bonaparte, ou la Princess Augusta.* Ze vun vere I 'ave not mooche troobal.

OFFICER.

You have already been of great service.

REYNARD.

Ze General vas pleased to recompense me.

OFFICER.

If you succeed you will receive high honors.

REYNARD.

If I *tomb* it vill be in ze service of my General and *La Belle France.* I 'ave not ze fear to die. Ze powaire zat support ze General vill protec' ze General's soldaire. I 'ave not ze fear to die. By Gar! I vas like to *pique* ze Barras vis my rappier!

[*Exeunt.*

SCENE SECOND.

PALACE OF SERBELLONI.

This scene is a large salon, divided into three rooms by marble columns. In room farthest back, a party of ladies and gentlemen. In middle room, JOSEPHINE *and party of ladies. In front room* BONAPARTE, EUGENE, AUGEREAU, *and other gentlemen, in conversation.*

BONAPARTE.

The Duke of Parma is unfortunate,
But left, where now he is, will do no harm,
And will no doubt serve well our purpose,
Carrying our every order to its end. ·
But, cut him off
And give his Dukedom to another,
And he will ever stir up strife and institute
Fresh intrigues. Here he can be useful made,
But elsewhere only hurtful.

AUGEREAU.

But he is a Bourbon, General,
A Bourbon!

BONAPARTE.

Well, then, he is a Bourbon—

Has nature therefore made him less for it?
Because three Bourbons have been killed in France,
Follows it that we must hunt the others down!
Proscriptions falling thus upon a name,
. A family, an entire class,
I never did and never will approve.
Cans't punish France for the crimes
Of the *Sans Culottes?* You say the Bourbons
Are the enemies of freedom; they were led
To the guillotine under a right
Which I do not acknowledge.

Enter ORIANI, *the astronomer, attended by Courtier.*

COURTIER.

The Proffesseur Oriani.

BONAPARTE.

We are indeed most happy, Professor,
That you do make one of our guests to-day.

ORIANI.

Ah, General, this magnificence
With which you are surrounded, dazzles me.

BONAPARTE.

Can it be such miserable splendors blind
A man who every night does contemplate

The far more lofty and impressive glories
Of the skies?

> [*Conducts him to 2d room and returns.*

Even Science bends before me.   *Aside.*]

Enter MANFREDINI (*attended by courtier*).

COURTIER.

Le Marquis Manfredini,
Ambassador of the Grand Duke of Tuscany.

BONAPARTE.

And can we serve your Grand Duke?

MANFREDINI.

Humbly our Grand Duke bows before
The greatest conqueror of Italy,
The General, most excellent, of France!
A fervent friendship sends he, greeting him,
And in sincerity will ever pray
He may find no less fame throughout the world
Than he already has so nobly won
In Italy.   Unto his sweet lady
‚He would his homage pay as at the shrine
Of every heavenly virtue—
Only regretting that affairs of state
Make his own presence here impossible.
Yet, through his ambassador, he begs -

You will your pleasure now convey to him
Regarding Tuscany.
For, though great confidence he entertains
In every good and noble quality
Of General Bonaparte, yet before power
There is always fear in breasts of those
Who stand so far beneath.
He would assurance, therefore humbly crave,
Of your good will.

BONAPARTE.

Signor Marquis :
You remind me of a certain creditor
Who once did importune, in modest phrase,
Coupled with flattery and confidence, .
The Cardinal de Rohan, " when he would ,
Be *kind* enough to pay him ? " " My dear sir,"
Said the Cardinal, " I pray you do not be
So very curious ! "
            [*Escorts him to second room—returns.*
Have given out that we transact no more
Of business to-day!   [*To Eugene.*

EUGENE.

The Ambassadors of Venice wait without.

.BONAPARTE.

Say that to Venice I will be an Atilla!
            [*Goes to second room.*

Now favor us with a sweet native air
Of Martinique!   [To Josephine.

JOSEPHINE.

First, pardon me, the great artist, LeGros,
Has been in waiting long, for my command
And your good pleasure, for a sitting—
Would you compel us to wait longer Mon Ami?
             [All retire to second room but JOSEPHINE
                         and BONAPARTE.

BONAPARTE.

For so great folly I have not the time—
No, no!   Another day.

JOSEPHINE.

             But you will not
Refuse a seat by my side?

BONAPARTE.

             Ah, no!   Never!
      [He sits.   JOSEPHINE beckons LEGROS.

             Enter LE GROS.
             [He commences the portrait.

BONAPARTE.

Excellent strategy!   But I will not
Endure it long.

JOSEPHINE.

Monsieur, would you surrender
Your position ?

BONAPARTE.

No, this artist's torment.

JOSEPHINE.

But if I should command ?

BONAPARTE.

I must obey.

JOSEPHINE.

A fair reply! so I release you.

BONAPARTE.

I 'd rather face a cannon's mouth.   [*Rises.*

JOSEPHINE.

To-morrow, good Le Gros, another sitting.
[*Exit* LE GROS.

Enter a COURTIER.

COURTIER.

The Princess Augusta.

BONAPARTE.

Attend her!
[*Exit* COURTIER.

Enter AUGUSTA (*attended*).

[COURTIER *goes to* EUGENE *in* 2d *room.*

COURTIER.

The Princess Augusta awaits you.

[*Returns with* EUGENE.　*Exit* COURTIER.

AUGUSTA.

Was never treason yet more base
Than that I now reveal to you?

BONAPARTE.

Impart.

AUGUSTA.

The plot was better laid than did appear
At first, and is in detail somewhat changed
Since our intelligence in France; Botot
Is superseded now by one who is
More crafty, dangerous, by far.

BONAPARTE.

Indeed !
How far have they progressed ?

AUGUSTA.

Not yet so far,
Thanks once again to Monsieur Botot.

Or rather to his weakness, but they may
Be easy taken in it.

JOSEPHINE.

Nay, we should say
Thanks to the Princess Augusta.

AUGUSTA.

But most
Is due to Madame Bonaparte.

BONAPARTE.

We are
Indebted to you both beyond all words.

JOSEPHINE.

No, not indebted, for there is no debt
When what we do is but for those we love!
Love only proves itself when it has reached
The last extremity for whom it loves,
And but receives its own when all is done
That may be possible.
—We did succeed in sending the despatch.
                                    [*To Augusta.*

AUGUSTA.

Your messenger was apprehended, ta'en.
No time must now be lost.

7

BONAPARTE.

They have not power—
No, not were all the world in league with them—
To harm us.   FATE sits supreme o'er all!
She will protect her son.

[*To Eugene.*   Please call a Courtier.

. [*Exit* EUGENE.

Re-enter EUGENE, *with* COURTIER.

[*To Courtier.*]   My secretaries!

[*Exit* COURTIER.

Re-enter COURTIER, *with three Secretaries.*

. [*Exit* COURTIER.

[*To* 1*st Sec.*]   Citizen Directors :
I owe you an open confession; my heart is de-
pressed and filled with horror through the constant
attacks of the Parisian journals.

[*To* 2*d Sec.*]   General Moreau :
Arrest at once Monsieur Botot and send to these
headquarters.

[*To* 1*st Sec.*]   Sold to the enemies of the republic; they rush upon me, who am boldly defending
the republic.

[*To* 3*d Sec.*]   General Joubert :
Your presence is needed at these headquarters.

[*To 1st Sec.*] I am "keeping the plunder" whilst I am defeating them; I "affect despotism," whilst I speak only as General-in-chief; I "assume supreme power," and yet I submit to law! Every thing I do is turned to crime against me; the poison streams over me.

[*To 2d Sec.*] Let him be attended closely but let no violence or insult be offered him.

[*To 1st Sec.*] Were any one in Italy to dare give utterance to the one-thousandth part of these calumnies, I would impose upon him an awful silence.

[*To 3d Sec.*] Set out at once, and travel with all possible haste.

[*To 1st Sec.*] In Paris, this is allowed to go on unpunished, and your tolerance is an encouragement. The Directory is thus producing the impression that it is opposed to me. If the Directors suspect me, let them say so, and I will justify myself. If they are convinced of my uprightness let them defend me.

[*To 2d Sec.*] Treat him indeed right civilly.

BONAPARTE.

[*To 1st Sec.*] In this circle of argument, I include the Directory with me, and cannot go beyond

it.   My desire is to be useful to my country. Must
I for reward drink the cup of poison?

[*To 3d Sec.*]   BONAPARTE.

[*To 2d Sec.*]   General Moreau :
                        Arrest at once and hold in
close confinement the friend of Botot, who recently arrived with him from France, wearing a
colonel's uniform.

[*To Augusta.*]   Of infantry?

AUGUSTA.
                        Of infantry.

BONAPARTE.
[*To 2d Sec.*]   Of infantry.

[*To 1st Sec.*]   I can no longer be satisfied with
empty, evasive arguments ; and if justice is not
done to me, then I must *take* it myself.

[*To 3d Sec.*]   General Marmont :
                        Arrest at once the Abbe
Sergi, and send to these headquarters.
                                    BONAPARTE.
[*To 2d Sec.*]   BONAPARTE.

[*To 3d Sec.*]   General Moreau :
                        Let no movement of
General Pichegru be unknown to you.   He is plot-
ting with the Bourbons.
                                    BONAPARTE.

[*To 1st Sec.*]   Therefore I am yours. Salutation
and brotherly love.

BONAPARTE.

[*To Eugene.*]   See that these despatches are sent
at once!

This artifice
That instigates employment of assassins—
Let them do their worst!   Yet we defy them!

Enter a COURTIER.

COURTIER.

The Count von Coblentz.

BONAPARTE.

Admit him!

Enter the COUNT VON COBLENTZ.

How now, another embassy?
I am tired of this vacillation,
Heartily!   In fourteen days will I dash
The Austrian monarchy to pieces
As I now break this.

(*Dashes cup to floor.*

[*To Eugene.*]   Say to the Archduke Charles,
In the name of General Bonaparte
All peace is at an end!

COBLENTZ. (*Falling to his knees.*

Mercy! Mercy!

BONAPARTE.

Ah!   Is Austria at my feet?
There may she rest in peace!

[*Curtain falls.*

END OF ACT III.

ACT IV.

SCENE FIRST.

PARIS.

Drawing-room of Compt de BARRAS — BARRAS *discovered sitting at table, rings. Several female pages answer.*

BARRAS.

Perdition catch my soul,
But you are beautiful! And yet have I
No time for you to-day, my merry birds!

(*Exeunt Pages.*

Stay, Stay, Marie! I had forgot my wine.

(*Marie brings wine. Exit.*

Bonaparte is yet far in advance,
In spite of me and mine. He marches on
As though the world were his. With cunning spies,
Sent to his very camp, I have beset him,
And yet no clue with which to humble him.
I strike him through the journals, strike him hard!
And Gohier helps me to trump up what lies
We think will be believed, but no avail.

And as his victories come heralded
I intercept reports to temper them ;
And yet, by some means, truth will leak, and
  through
The streets no sound is heard but that same damned
Inexorable worn out yell
"*Vive le* Bonaparte!"
By Jove! 'fore this " Achilles" we have proved
But puny Trojans.

Enter—GOHIER *and* MOULINS.

(*Cries without of "Vive le Bonaparte!" etc.*)

What means this, Gohier!   Are the people mad ?

GOHIER.

The streets e'en now throng with the multitude,
Splitting their lungs with " Vive le Bonaparte!"
And yet 't is scarce an hour since his coming.

MOULINS.

He will be troublesome ;—His Montebello
Has not left an impress easily removed.
Dam-me, but they made a king of him,
And to his wife more princely homage gave
Than she should have as Empress of the French.

GOHIER.

And Venice wrought herself to such ado
As he had been an emperor.

BARRAS.

[Offering filled glasses.
How comes it that he does so soon arrive?

GOHIER.

You know he ever unexpected comes—
'T is thus he wins his victories.

MOULINS.

He 'll have a victory here to win, or we.

BARRAS.

Well said, Monsieur Moulins!
Nor can we long delay.   This blazing brand
Of glory he has snatched fires all hearts,
And will illume the world unless put out.
Saw you his letter citing us our duty
Respecting the late journals that some truths
Do tell of him?   I think he 'd dictate terms
To Heaven for his own reception.

GOHIER.

And undertake a battle with the hosts
Of Michael an' they did not cry " vive ! vive !"
I heard of this great document, and think
It is damned impudent, to put it mildly.
—I understand his next great field of fame
Is Egypt.

BARRAS *and* MOULINS.

Egypt?

GOHIER.

Longs to carve his name
On the great pyramids !

BARRAS.

We'll let him carve!

MOULINS.

Yes, we will let him carve.

BARRAS.

Monsieur Gohier, 'tis the right place for him.
Art sure he has this new ambition ?

GOHIER.

That he has so expressed it, I am sure.

BARRAS.

What say you? We will take him at his word,
Before to repent the thought is left him.
And if he meet successes in the East
As he has done in Italy, I'll say
He can have France. Egypt! Ha! ha! ha! Egypt—

A health to the campaign in Egypt!

ALL (*drinking.*)

E-g-y-p-t!

BARRAS.

But we must make some demonstration
To receive him now, or the good people
Will suspect us.

GOHIER.

Yes, he must be received
By the Directory, and publicly.

BARRAS.

Was 't not enough
That all the most high potentates,
Whereunto he did come, should do him homage?
Nay, seek him where he graciously permitted?
Gods! they did squander gold in heaps
Upon the palace Serbelloni!
It was a rival for the Tuileries!
All Italy
And the nobility of Lombardy
Vied with each other who should humblest be—
Even the Grand Duke of Tuscany,
Brother of the Emperor.
Then followed Montebello in the train,
Seeking to overtop all rivalry!

And Venice, to appease him, made his wife
A veritable queen!   Jove, what magnificence!
I wonder they made not a bonfire
Of their town for her!—Now, he to Paris comes,
Borne as world's conqueror amidst a sea
Of crazy-witted fools, whose rotten breaths
Join in acclaim that rolls in mighty waves
Before him!   And we his way with roses
Needs must strew, else lose our place—perchance
Our heads.

MOULINS.

If we lose not our heads, at best—

BARRAS.

What!   Fear you?   We will trip him yet—
Look you! we will now give him such applause
As circumstances may demand, and *I*
Will receive him—*embrace* him if need be,
That they may see how we do *love* him,
And then in Egypt offer him a field
Where he shall *carve* unto his soul's content.
But if he do return as now he comes
He other wits must thank than Barras' for 't.

GOHIER.

Well said, good Barras.   Now, by my soul!
This smacks of glorious enterprise!

A health to Egypt and the Pyramids!
Where we'll provide for this "Prince Bonaparte"
An Eastern Empire—six feet by two!

[They drink.

BARRAS.

There's little interest for us without ;
Tarry, and we will test the strength of this
More thoroughly.

Enter—A PAGE.

PAGE.

General Bonaparte and Eugene de Beauharnias.

Enter BONAPARTE *and* EUGENE.

[Exit Page.

BONAPARTE.

How now?   Have we surprised you, gentlemen?

BARRAS.

An honor that we do appreciate.

GOHIER *and* MOULINS.

Yes—

BARRAS.

Your absence wore right heavily—

MOULINS.

Yes—

GOHIER.

We did regret your quick departure—

MOULINS.

Yes—

BONAPARTE.

Peace!
Have done this shallow-pated stuff!

BARRAS.

                                        We wait
The pleasure of our *guests!*

BONAPARTE.

                        Nay, upon that
I am not sensitive.   Necessity
Is law, and courtesy demands no more
Than this; or, if it does, will e'er be found
A weak competitor.   Touching the matter
For our consideration for to-night,
Can Monsieur Barras, or his friend Gohier,
Or yet Moulins, inform us as to what
The business was of Monsieur Botot
In Italy, by whom sent, paid by whom?

BARRAS.

You are beyond me, General.

BONAPARTE.

No doubt!

GOHIER.

And me.

MOULINS.

And me.

BONAPARTE.

Beyond you all, no doubt!
But come, to the purpose!

BARRAS.

To what purpose?

BONAPARTE.

To *no* purpose, it would appear, unless
You are more direct.   Come now, the question!

BARRAS.

What question?

BONAPARTE.

Touching Monsieur Botot.

BARRAS.

Ah, since you have reminded me, I think,
The Government *did* send Monsieur Botot
Upon some secret service.

MOULINS.

Yes, you're right.

BONAPARTE.

The Government?   What department of it?

BARRAS.

What else than the Directory?

BONAPARTE.

Indeed!
What members of it?   Come, impart!

BARRAS.

We do not catch your meaning.

BONAPARTE.

Nor *catch* you me!
Your memory is torpid, 'twould appear!
Now this is something quite remarkable!
Perhaps, then, one of you may be prepared
To explain why your Monsieur Barras,

But two short days ago, had business
In secret council with a Chouan chief,
Whom he did entertain right royally,
As more befits a prince.
Or if your ignorance in this should prove
As in the matter of Monsieur Botot—
Since ignorance becomes proverbial
Sometimes, and follows in unbroken chain,
As doth the matter called in evidence—
You may refresh your minds with this and this,
And tell me what you think would be the fate—
Should be the fate—of those intriguers base
Who offered to betray their General—
The General of *France*—and give him o'er
To Beaulieu?

BARRAS.

        Would you hold us for these reports
Made by our enemies and yours? Of this
Of which you speak we are most innocent.

BONAPARTE.

Speak you for all?—So, I understand you.
—The secret service of Monsieur Botot,
And other secret service of like nature,
Are known as well to me as the base hearts
Who did employ in it. The potent means
By which I have been thoroughly informed,

8

Tell me of secret conclaves, dark designs,
And weak schemes numberless, to overthrow
My power, yet all have fallen harmless,
As all *must* fall who are opposed to me.

BARRAS.

What we could do we have done to expose
These villainies.

GOHIER.

.   Yes, we have done our best
To circumvent them, here and everywhere.

MOULINS.

Indeed we have, you are quite right, we have.

BONAPARTE.

Can it be possible?   Why Beauharnais,
Look you upon these men !   Duplicity
Ne'er had a name till now! oh precious knaves !
But, see ! their faces like as ours do bear
The stamp of immortality !   How calm!
Was ever innocence protected
By more placid mien ? ` Yet are these the same,
The self same traitors, .who sat in council,
Less than an hour ago to ruin me.
This is that same Barras who would embrace
And fawn upon me when I did return !
And these, his creatures, weak and pliable.

BARRAS.

Beware! The voice of the Directory—
The great Directory of France—does rest
In those you have accused—Look well to it!

BONAPARTE.

What! Threat you me before my very face?
Why, here is now assurance worth a cause!
"Beware!" Ye gods! What impudence!
"Beware!" Why, Beauharnais, this is a feast
Beyond comparison!
When 'neath the shadow of the Pyramids
We'll have this to refresh us, this "Beware!"

BARRAS.

We've had enough of this!

EUGENE.

That's easy proved—[*draws.*

[BARRAS *draws.*

BONAPARTE.   [*To Eugene.*

What!
When did you fall so low that you would put
Yourself against such rotten carrion?
Austria would refuse to cross your sword
Wearing such blood upon it!
Hear we now (*to Directors*),

—Ye miserable hangers-on of time!
Ye *would-be* arch conspirators,
But that ye lack conception for it.—
The affairs of State, or War's swift enterprise,
Wherein fair genius ànd the strongest wins,
I leave you as before.   Malign as you will;
Join all the arts of Mephistopheles
Unto your own, lo! I *defy* you!
'Tis not within the power of man to harm me!
But hark ye now!
There is one point where I am vulnerable;
This has been touched by your vile, slanderous
      tongues!
For other cause, with this surprise, ye never
Had been honored.
I use few words, you know me!—
If I do trace to you another word, a look,
Or aught that shall in any way reflect
Upon the fair name of my family,
Now hear!—
By the great God, I swear, I'll visit you
With vengeance swift as my wrath!
So farewell!

        (*Exit* EUGENE *and* BONAPARTE.

        BARRAS.

            Can Carbon and St. Rejeant
Be ready within the hour?

GOHIER.

Let us confer
With them,

BARRAS.

By every god I swear I will not sleep
Till he is done for.

[*Exeunt.*

SCENE SECOND.

A STREET IN PARIS.

BARRAS *and* GOHIER *discovered.*

BARRAS.

Is all ready?

GOHIER.

Waiting but his coming.

BARRAS.

Then shall we see
If that his goddess will protect him now.
Carbon and St. Rejeant, are they paid?

GOHIER.

Not till the work is done.

BARRAS.

That is well thought !
Who will apply the fuse?

GOHIER.

St. Rejeant's self.

BARRAS.

The place?

GOHIER.

The Rue St. Nicaise.

BARRAS.

Can they fail?

GOHIER.

I hardly think it possible, as they—
Carbon and Limœlan—will watch
The progress of the Consul's carriage
As it shall leave the Tuileries, until
The time to give the signal to St. Rejeant.

BARRAS.

Let us be gone !   The hour approaches!
We must not be seen.

[*Exeunt.*

[*As they go off a rumbling noise is heard*

*followed by the appearance of the guard
and carriage of* BONAPARTE. — *The
scene then changes to the Rue St. Nicaise, where a cart is discovered with
the infernal machine in it; a little
girl holding the horse, and* ST. RE-
JEANT *off at one side.—The carriage
passes—after which an explosion.—
Scene changes back; carriage passing
safely away.*

GOHIER.

He did escape us.

BARRAS.

But all the powers of hell shall not save him!
God! how his words do rankle yet in me!
Now to our wits and the new enterprise—
We 'll find no time for napping from this out.
Monsieur Gohier, art certain of your chief?
These Chouans are as unreliable
As desperate.

GOHIER.

Fear not! I know my man.
Besides our gold, he's wedded to our cause
By an old grudge against the General.
Such men forget offences only when

They are revenged.   Seemed he not ready
When you spoke to him?

BARRAS.

                    Too much so, I thought.
The fellow had his plans all quite matured ;
He was too zealous.   Plans so well defined
Suggested to my mind a counter plot,
Having its origin in subtler brains.

GOHIER.

Oh, never fear, I know him well!
You must in this my better judgment trust.
He will requite us all.

BARRAS.

                    Why, he did know
The very day on which our Georges came !
And Biville cliff was as well known to him
As my chateau to me.

GOHIER.

                    Most certain 'tis,
And every dangerous path
Between Dieppe and Treport he knows as well.

BARRAS.

He saw the very cable from the cliff,

Descending through the cleft unto the sea ;
Saw Georges seize it, and then, by its aid
Climb up the precipice.   Then, in their turn,
Each of his followers.

GOHIER.

Why should he not ?
Since he of that same passage has, for years,
Been a most constant warder.

BARRAS.

Can it be ?
Why did you not impart all this before ?

GOHIER.

Matters of graver moment took its place.
What says the General Pichegru
Touching Moreau ?

BARRAS.

He finds him more ready
Than pliable.

GOHIER.

I do not understand.

BARRAS.

Moreau shuffles, cuts and deals for Moreau.

GOHIER.

What, stands he not with us?

BARRAS.

               Only so far
As we do stand with him.   In his own glass,
Fondly presuming that it is the world,
He gazes steadily, seeing himself,
Himself alone, and cannot understand
Why this great central figure stands not out,
In bold relief to others as himself.
Another meeting is appointed now
With Georges, at his safe retreat, Chaillot.
'Tis hoped an understanding to secure.
But poor Riviere is driven to despair,
And talks but of the apathy of France.

GOHIER.

He lacks in courage and tenacity.
Were't not for Madame Bonaparte, I'd chance
A fortune on our quick success.   But she
Has half the eyes of Paris after us,
And, for herself, I think she never sleeps.
But see!   The dawn already is upon us!
We must be gone.

                                [*Exeunt.*

Enter, from either side, CITIZENS.

1ST CITIZEN.

Vive la Consulate!   Vive le Bonaparte!

2D CITIZEN.

What now, good friend, what news?

1ST CITIZEN.

Bonaparte is made first Consul!   And for life!
Vive la Consulate!

ALL.

Vive la Consulate!   Vive le Bonaparte!

2D CITIZEN.

But this sudden change, tell us how came it?

1ST CITIZEN.

Ever as he wins, by strategy.   He has over-
thrown his enemies in the Directory and Consulate.

2D CITIZEN.

And our enemies!—the enemies of France.

1ST CITIZEN.   (*Singing.*)

He will give us peace and plenty—peace and
plenty.   Vive le Bonaparte!

ALL.   (*Singing*).

He will make smile the land of France. Vive
le Bonaparte! Vive le Bonaparte!

> [*Exeunt, singing.*

SCENE THIRD.

The Council of the Five Hundred.—Lucien Bonaparte *presiding.*

(*Confusion.*)

GOHIER.

Citizen President:
We must a new election hold at once!
There hangs no less upon it than the fate
Of the Republic.

1st MEMBER.

No! Such haste but shows
Base cowardice!

2d MEMBER.

Shame! Shame! Shame!

> [*Cheers on the right.*

3d MEMBER.

Such language
Is an insult to the Council!

> [*Cheers on the left.*

THE PRESIDENT.

This must cease
Or we will end in anarchy.

GOHIER.

I rise to ask the member if his charge
Of cowardice means to apply to men
Or measures?

1ST MEMBER.

To both.

GOHIER.

Then I do hurl it back
And challenge to a test!

(*Great confusion.*)

BARRAS.

This is madness!
Are we devoid of reason? Hear, oh hear!
Who is to profit by this senseless strife?
The Great Republic? No! Nor you, nor I,
Nor either of our factions! Such a course
Can in destruction only end
Of all! Who seeks the good of this, our France!

1ST MEMBER.

Not Barras!

3D MEMBER.

Shame! Shame!

1ST MEMBER.

Conspirator!
Behold the arch conspirator!

VOICES.

Conspirator!   Conspirator!

1ST MEMBER.

Tell us of Georges, and the Chouans
Whom you employed to murder Bonaparte!

BARRAS.

I ask again,
Who seeks the good of this, our France? Let him
Propose a sacrifice that he will make,
And I will clasp his hand and go with him
To his extremest measure—even death!
What then are we through passion, to lose all?
In this extremity we are but ripe
For anarchy.   Ho, Patriots! Would you feel
The Despot's iron yoke upon your necks!
The usurper comes by stealthy strides,
And even now is at our gates!

Enter BONAPARTE *and* EUGENE.

Sec! See!
Even at the word he comes!   Away with him !

3D MEMBER.

Down with him !

ANOTHER MEMBER.

~He is a traitor!

ANOTHER MEMBER.

Cromwell!

SEVERAL VOICES.

Down with the usurper!

BONAPARTE.

Citizens, hear me!

VOICES.

Down with him!   Traitor!   Traitor!   Usurper!

BONAPARTE.

Will you not hear me ?

VOICES.

No!   No!   Down with him!

[*They rush towards him.* EUGENE *has sig-
naled the Grenadiers at the door, who
now surround him.*

A VOICE.

Down with the usurper! He brings soldiers
To overawe us!

BONAPARTE.

Who loves me, let him follow me!

[*Marches out guarded by the Grenadiers.—
Shouts without—Vive le* BONAPARTE!

BONAPARTE (*at the door*).

Protect the President of the Five Hundred!

[*Exit.*

[EUGENE *and Grenadiers
march in and escort the President out.*

END OF ACT IV.

ACT V.

SCENE FIRST.

NOTRE DAME—THE CORONATION.

PANTOMIME.

Upon the opening of this scene is discovered the interior of Notre Dame, decorated with unequaled magnificence.

The throne of the Emperor and Empress represents a monument within a monument, between two columns, supporting a pediment, upon which is a representation of the crown of Charlemange.

On the left is seen the throne designed for the Pope, over which is a pediment supporting a diamond cross.

Directly in front of either throne, in the centre of the stage, is the Altar on which are seen the Scepter, the Sword and the Imperial crowns.

Prelates are discovered on either side of the throne designed for the Pope. The Bonaparte

9

family on either side of the throne of the Emperor and Empress.

At the right of the stage, dignitaries of State.

Enter POPE PIUS VII.

He approaches the altar, kneels, then ascends his throne!—The Prelates approach and salute him.

Enter NAPOLEON *and* JOSEPHINE.

They approach the altar and kneel—Pope descends from his throne, comes to altar, holds his hands over them in blessing.

Napoleon raises his head and is annointed by Pope on forehead, arms and hands. Pope then takes sword—Napoleon rises—Pope holds sword as if in blessing, then girds it on Napoleon.

Pope offers to take crown, but Napoleon quickly reaches it himself and deliberately places it upon his own head. He then takes the crown of the Empress, and, as she is still kneeling beside him, places it gently on her head ; then taking her by the hand, she arises.

Pope then blesses scepter and gives to Napoleon. The Emperor and Empress ascend their throne. Pope advances to the foot of the throne and raises his hands in benediction.

SCENE II.]   *Napoleon and Josephine.*   131

SCENE SECOND.

PALACE IMPERIAL.

THE EMPEROR'S CABINET, *dimly illuminated.*

NAPOLEON *discovered.*

NAPOLEON.

Thus far has Fate the firm alliance kept,
Thus far through scenes of fratricidal strife,
And bloody, devastating, frightful war,
From conquering to conquer led her son!
Till now great France and all her power, lands,
Rivers, seas, immensity of wealth,
And teeming millions of brave chivalry,
Are but the subjects of his scepter's sway!
—But oh, great Goddess! at what price is this!
Unto that last dark, dismal sleep, thou'st sent
Unnumbered hecatombs of human forms,
From which to raise this sad renown!
The sighs, the tears, the anguish of despair,
The body's torture and the soul's defeat,
The wailing millions of a world attest!
Oh Goddess! Who can measure that great cup,
Wherein has been contained the sorrow's depth
Which thou hast forced the world to drink for him?
Eternity alone!
—And soon there will come, even for *thy* son

The end that is decreed for all.   To sleep
That long last sleep, which goes forever on
Without a dream!   Goddess, where then thy son?
On whom shall the Imperial mantle fall?
Childless, thou leavest him to reign alone!
Across the dark abyss of death, no tie!
—I *did* defy all power for Josephine,
And is the penalty her barren womb?
—If not in my offspring, how shall my blood
And hers commingle on the throne of France?
Yet 'tis decreed; reveal the mystery!
—Nay, then, do gods combine gainst Thee and me,
To overthrow my power?
O'er Thee may none prevail!
Bear then, swift as His lightnings,
E'en to the great throne of the Thunderer,
Defiance!
So let our bond become inseparable;
Subdue the Immortals Thou, the Earth
Leave unto me!
—Now will I *bridge* the chasm over death!
My scepter's power shall rule throughout the world,
And my own blood shall reign upon the throne,
In spite of gods!—aye, though it cost me
Josephine!

Enter JOSEPHINE.

[*He rushes to and embraces her.*

Josephine! my peerless, peerless one!

JOSEPHINE.

Didst thou call me?
—Wherefore with voice so wild and sorrowful?

NAPOLEON.

A hell of ugly dreams environed me—
Thou wilt not leave me?

JOSEPHINE.

No! Never! Never!
My noble one, knowest thou not my love?

NAPOLEON.

Yes!—yes!—
Lead me away—I would have rest.

[Exeunt.

Enter EUGENE *and* AUGUSTA.

EUGENE.

And this—and this is greatness!

AUGUSTA.

Ah, yes!
But are you the happier, my husband?

EUGENE.

No! let me confess it, no, Augusta!

In the attaining, not in the thing attained,
Our happiness does come.   The soul's unrest
Cannot be satisfied.

AUGUSTA.

May it not pause
To dwell with rapture on a great success?

EUGENE.

Not the truly great soul, no!   It cannot!
To pause were death, and, being immortal,
It cannot die, therefore it may not pause.

AUGUSTA.

But we have reached a careful height,
So, let us bask us in our glory's sun ;
Nor let Ambition's tempting voice betray
Us into paths which, though they lead to fame,
Power, place, but leave us the sure mark
For base intrigue and treachery.

EUGENE.

Ah! Ah !
What wondrous potency is in that voice!

AUGUSTA.

If so, why should you sigh and knit your brow?

EUGENE.

My sigh was for the Empress, not her son;
And when I heard your voice I thought if she
Possessed such power with the Emperor,
He could not—

AUGUSTA.

Has he declared his policy?

EUGENE.

No, not in words.

AUGUSTA.

By act, then?   Tell me all!

EUGENE.

Not by act.   Heaven save us from that hour!
—I left my mother a short hour ago;
She had sent for me, and, when I met her,
Fell upon my neck and, weeping bitterly,
Told me she could no longer hope; bade me
Try, with her, to be resigned in feeling
That our great loss was the great gain of France.

AUGUSTA.

Has he then signified as much to her?

EUGENE.

She but divines it from his manner.

AUGUSTA.

Is he unkind?

EUGENE.

No, no! demonstrative
In kindness—pets and caresses her
As though 'twere but a little day preceding
A long absence; and in an hundred other ways
Betrays himself.

AUGUSTA.

Alas, poor Empress!

EUGENE.

This interview and my unhappy dream
Have left me almost fitted for despair.

AUGUSTA.

A dream?

EUGENE.

Last night I dreamed our Paris was besieged;
I, second in command, had been to inspect
Our outposts. The night wore on towards morning,
When a sound as of the distant roaring
Of artillery, drew my attention
To the south and east.—The heavens, all cloudless,
Were glorious with stars!—Louder, deeper,

The terrible reverberations rolled,
Nearer, until the very dome of heaven
Seemed to tremble! Then, through the vaulted
    azure
Rushed chariots of war, drawn by fierce steeds,
Whose dilate nostrils sent forth the lightnings!
Until the sun, from out a sea of blood,
Leaped forth, a wild world of fire!
The Emperor, with folded arms, the while
Strode to and fro upon the parapet,
Regarding silently.   But, as the sun
Came forth, he stumbled, fell, and upon me,
Who stood beneath, without the battlements.

AUGUSTA.

Nay! Nay! Be not cast down! 'T was but a
    dream!

EUGENE.

Ah, yes! 't was but a dream!—It is the hour
When Reynard should arrive.

AUGUSTA.

Whence comes he?

EUGENE.

Berlin.

AUGUSTA.

His English is amusing, and, besides,
His repartee is excellent, and will
Divert your mind, I trust, for you must not
So constantly brood o'er this matter.

Enter REYNARD.

Welcome, Reynard!

REYNARD.

Reynard is proud of such velcome!

EUGENE.

Of one so faithful we may well be proud.

REYNARD.

I am glad to report zat I make ze success in Berlin.

AUGUSTA.

Bravo, good Reynard! you shall have reward.

REYNARD.

Ze ladie smile is my good recompense!

EUGENE.

You, it seems, are always happy, Reynard.

REYNARD.

I 'ave not vat you call ze greatness, zen I am vis-out ze care—I 'ave ze content vis ze world; I no can make it ovaire.

AUGUSTA.

Were you ever in love, Reynard?

REYNARD.

In loafe? *Oui, oui,* many times! Ha! ha! many times!

AUGUSTA.

Not very deep?

REYNARD.

I no 'ave ze vat you call—ze loafe sick.

AUGUSTA.

Indeed! How, then, have you escaped?

REYNARD.

La Belle France 'ave ze plaintie, Madamoselle! Ver plaintie!

AUGUSTA.

You *are* a philosopher. But did you never love one beyond all others?

REYNARD.

Sometimes, for ze little vile.

AUGUSTA.

You are indeed mankind in miniature.

REYNARD.

Zis loafe make ze conscience pliable. I loafe all ze Madamoselle.

AUGUSTA.

You are generous!

REYNARD.

I must not offend.

AUGUSTA.

Oh, no—no offense! But you are a strange fellow.

REYNARD.

Ven I may serve you, I vill 'ave ze great pleasure—

AUGUSTA.

This needs no further proof, good Reynard.

EUGENE.

Have you orders from the Emperor following this from Berlin?

REYNARD.

Zis is all.

EUGENE.

Have you reported ?

REYNARD.

I 'ave send ze report by ze Secretaire. Zen ze Emperor send for me, zat he vould like to see me. But ven I vas come in ze presence he 'ave ze ver sad look. He vas speak ver plaisant, but I 'ave ze fear zat he vas not please vis me—he 'ave ze cloud in ze face.

EUGENE.

Do not let this trouble you. The Emperor is in trouble touching an affair of State diplomacy. He entertains for you only the kindest regards, I assure you.

REYNARD.

Zen I am happie !

EUGENE.

Would I could say as much !

[*Exit* EUGENE *and* AUGUSTA.

REYNARD.

Zere is somezing ze mattaire. Ah! ze great man 'ave alvays ze troubal. By Gar ! I would not give ze content of Reynard for ze crown of ze Emperor.

[*Exit.*

SCENE THIRD.

EMPEROR'S PRIVATE PARLORS.

NAPOLEON *discovered asleep*—JOSEPHINE *sitting by his side.*

JOSEPHINE.

In thy soft arms,
Oh, hold him tenderly! sweet, gentle sleep!
Hover above him, spirits of the blest,
On waves Æolian, and touch his soul
With your divinest symphonies!   O'er him
Let Lethe's spray in dewy showers fall;
The while may rays of Hope shine through, and
    show
A bow of promise on the heavy clouds
That now shut out my heaven!—Oh, noble brow!
Realm of fair Genius!   throne of a lofty soul!
Ah, could I lift thy sorrow, as I lift
These locks so silken, soft!—Oh, splendid orbs!
Where rests your glory now?   It cannot sleep!
—Ah, pale, pale cheek!   Thou art quite colorless!
Oh, precious lips! on ye, my soul shall melt
In this one kiss!
—This hand, I press to my poor heart, would wield
The scepter of the world!   But at what cost!
Ah, *can* it put away its Josephine!
Oh God!   I can but weep!   [*Exit.*

(*Napoleon starts out of his dream.*)

NAPOLEON.

Aye! Aye!   In spite of gods!
Had every god the power of mighty Jove,
All leagued against my cause, yet will I sway
The scepter of the world!   I will!   I will!
I will!   'Tis I—NAPOLEON !

(*Thunder.*)

Turn loose
Your thunderbolts of wrath !   Bellow and roar!
Upheave the earth!   Unlock the vaults of hell!
Reveal the seething cauldrons of the damned!
The Indomitable Will *defies* you!
. . . .   What dreams torment my soul!
Ah! will they drive me mad?—Once more I wake—
The sombre shadows sleep—No wave of sound—
My brain reels !   Is this death ?
. . . .   Ah—wondrous, incomparable pageantry!
What grand procession this of stately forms—
The marshalled glory of the Universe!
—All-wise! All-mighty! All-foreseeing Jove!
Thou, who in thunder tones command'st the host
August, of the Immortals, hail! all hail!
What holdest thou in keeping for the great ?
Silence!
—Thou of the silver bow, Far-seeing
Phœbus Apollo, shall *we* be gods ?

—Pallas, Minerva, answer me, and tell
What life awaits beyond the tomb.
—Oh, Fate, my mother, thou dost sit supreme
O'er all! Speak! Oh, speak!—All, all is silence!
'Tis gone!
—What marvelous perfection passes now!
A crown of thorns, and in His hands and side
Are wounds;—I know Him not!—But see! who
    follows,
Worshipping?—Josephine!—Alone! Alone!—
On earth and in Eternity!

                                        [*Exit.*

Enter REYNARD.

REYNARD.

Ah ha! Mon Dieu! Somezing is ze mattaire—
ze vorld 'ave turn ze wrong vay! Ough!—Le Dia-
ble!—Reynard vas scare at ze self—somezing is ze
mattaire—Reynard vill be no longaire ze valet—
he mus' go avay vis ze self. Ough! hell sacrament!
—By gar! I vill go avay soom plaise!—Ah! Mon
Dieu! Reynard mus' not lose ze mind—he mus'
'ave ze *sang froid*—he mus' be ze leetle fox! Ah
ha!—By gar! Reynard, ze fox, he know somezing!
Vat he know?—He know vat Reynard ze valet
know!—Reynard ze valet tell Reynard ze fox!—
Vat he tell?—Vat he see vis ze eye an ze ear!—
Ah ha!—Ze Emperor talk vis ze gods in ze tun-

daire!—Sooblime conceptione !—Magnifique!—He
is vun brave General!—He no 'ave ze fear!—He is
ze graand Napoleon!—Reynard mus' be ze leetle
fox!

Enter EUGENE.

EUGENE.

Why, Reynard, what is the matter ?

REYNARD.

Ze mattaire? Ah ha! Ze leetle fox mus' not
tell vat he know.

EUGENE.

But to me, your friend !

REYNARD.

Reynard mus' be true to ze friend ?

EUGENE.

Always!

REYNARD.

Zen he mus' be true to ze Emperor!

EUGENE.

I do not ask you to betray confidence.

10

REYNARD.

Ven I see and 'ear somezing, zat is ze confidence.
By Gar, I must be true to my General!

EUGENE.

But is it not best we should know?

REYNARD.

Ah, Mon Dieu! I mus' 'ave ze time to t'ink. Ze
Emperor 'ave ze great troubal!—he vas talk vis ze
gods in ze tundair. He is vun graand Emperor.

EUGENE.

Alas! My mother!—The Empress comes, let us
withdraw.

Exit REYNARD *and* EUGENE.

Re-enter JOSEPHINE.

JOSEPHINE.

Oh, Siren Hope!
No more! No more! Else tune your lyre to a dirge!
Nay, lure me on to death! but let me die
Mid mournful strains! Sweet music is for those
Who live, or here or on the other side,
But for the dying, sing a requiem!
—Ah, your soft voice has touched my trusting
    heart

So oft, that now the touch does wound, where once
It had the power to heal! Peace! Away!
—Now, now am I alone! E'en Hope is gone!
Oh last, oh dearest, sweetest, only comfort
When the heart is crushed—to be alone!
—Come now, my soul, and we will sit us down
And nurse our loneliness.

(She sits on the floor.)

Oh, Grief: thou art the only heir that I could bear!
I hold thee to my breast! Now feed and take
The life that gave thee life! Oh baby, mine,
Thou was't brought forth in pain, thou givest pain
In nursing, yet I hug thee close, for thou
Was't born of *him*! My only treasure thou!
And thou wil't not depart! And none will take
Thee from me; there is no one covets thee.
Thou art unwelcome everywhere but here—
Here on thy mother's breast. Oh visit not
Thy father! Let him forget thee, forget
That thou was't born of him!—Thy lips are cold,
They chill me to the heart! Cold, cold thy form!
Cold as dead love! Cold as thy father's love!
—No! No! His love is not cold!
Thy father's love is not cold, baby, no!
He loves me, oh, he loves me as his soul!
—But oh, he does not know how thou has't grown,
Feeding upon the currents of my life,
Feeding upon the currents of my life,

Until thou art so heavy, hard to bear!
He does not know!   Ah!· Ah!—He shall not
   know!
For thou art not so heavy as his world—
His world!—But *mine ?* He was my world—He *is!*
              [*Rising.*]
I cannot, cannot give him up!   No!   No!
Give him to another!   God!   Oh God!—
   [*going*]—Thou cling'st so close, my baby!
Nay, feed on!—Where shall we go, my baby ?
Feed on!   Feed on!
                       [*Exit.*

          Re-enter NAPOLEON.

    He sits at table—paper and writing ma-
       terial before him.   He takes up pen
       to write.   The pen drops from his hand.

             NAPOLEON.

            [*Looking upon his hand.*

Thou wouldst not tremble so
To sign thy death-warrant!—Thou hast been firm,
Unfaltering, mid battles' din and roar,
And frightful cries of souls crushed out of men!
When, to write one word, the voice of armies
Spoke the doom of states!   Yea, when that one
   word

Would send brave thousands, human lives, to
    death!
But one word, a name, 't is easy writ—

NAPOLEON!   [*Re-takes pen.*

Eternity resolved into a drop!
Ah, little world, thou tremblest on the point!
Black, black as death! No light illumes thee now,
But it will come!
—Now, little world, thou 'lt be the word, a name
That shall be crown and halo to the earth!
So 't is decreed!—
God! It has fallen! My world is shattered!
Light has gone out forever!
.... Why, this is madness! Am I, then, so weak?-
Is this Napoleon?—The arm of Fate,
The hand that holds the destiny of France,
Should bear a steadier nerve!
Ah, thou hast shown thy loyalty
To Josephine!—Now what thou ow'st to France!

                  [*Writes.*

'T is done!

                     [*Exit.*

SCENE FOURTH.

EMPEROR'S CABINET.

JOSEPHINE *is discovered attended by* AUGUSTA *and*
HORTENSE.

Enter NAPOLEON,

Attended by EUGENE, *the* KING *and* QUEEN OF
NAPLES, *the* KING *and* QUEEN OF WESTPHALIA,
the PRINCESS BORGHESE, *the* CHANCELLOR CAM-
BACERES *and* COUNT REGNAUD DE SAINT JEAN
D'ANGEL. *The two latter as* OFFICIERS DE
L'ETAT CIVIL *for the Imperial family.*
NAPOLEON *advances to* JOSEPHINE—*speaks to her.*
She comes down the stage, supported by AUG-
USTA *and* HORTENSE.

NAPOLEON. (*Reads.*)

"MY COUSIN, PRINCE ARCH-CHANCELLOR :—I
sent you a closed letter of this day's date, ordering
you to present yourself in my cabinet, that I might
make known to you the resolution which I and the
Empress, my own dear spouse, have come to. I
was very glad that the kings, queens and princesses,
my brothers and sisters, my brothers-in-law and
sisters-in-law, my step-daughter and step-son, become my adopted son, should be present at what I
had to make known to you.

The policy of my monarchy, the interest and
necessity of my peoples, which have constantly

guided all my actions, require that I should leave
after me to children, inheritors of my love for my
people, this throne on which Providence has placed
me. For many years, however, I have lost the
hope of having children by my marriage with my
well beloved spouse, the Empress Josephine; this
it is that induces me to sacrifice the dearest affec-
tions of my heart, to hearken only to the good of
the State, and desire the dissolution of our marriage.

Arrived at the age of forty, I conceive the hope
of living long enough to bring up after my own
mind and my own views, the children it shall
please Providence to give me. God knows how
much such a resolution has cost my heart; but
there is no sacrifice too great for my courage, when
it is demonstrated to me that it is for the good of
France. I cannot conclude without saying, that
far from having ever had reason to complain, I
have, on the contrary, only encomiums to bestow
on the attachment and tenderness of my well-be-
loved spouse. She has embellished fifteen years of
my life; the memory of this will always remain
engraved on the memory of my heart. She has
been crowned by my hand; it is my desire that
she retain the rank and title of Empress, but above
all, that she never doubt my sentiments, and that
she always hold me for her best and dearest friend.

JOSEPHINE. —[*reads.*]

" With the permission—

[*Hands MS. to M. Regnaud.*]

REGNAUD [*reads.*]

" With the permission of my august and dear

spouse, I must declare, that retaining no hope öf
having children who may satisfy the requirements
of his policy and the interests of France, I have
pleasure in giving him the greatest proof of attachment and devotedness that was ever given on earth.
I owe all to his bounty; it was his hand that
crowned me, and on his throne I have received only
manifestations of affection and love from the French
people.

I think, to evince my gratitude for all these
sentiments, in consenting to the dissolution of a
marriage which is now an obstacle to the good of
France, which deprives it of the happiness of being
one day governed by the descendants of a great
man, so evidently raised up by Providence, to efface
the evils of a terrible revolution, and to re-estab-
the altar, the throne and social order. But the dissolution of my marriage will make no change in
the sentiments of my heart—in me the Emperor
will always have his best friend! I know how
much this act, commanded by policy, and by such
great interests, has rent his heart, but we both of
us glory in the sacrifice which we make to the
good of the country."

(JOSEPHINE *falls.*)

JOSEPHINE.

(NAPOLEON, *with folded arms, regarding her.*)

At last! At last!
The end has come. .And now I pass beyond
Those scenes where, with our happiness,
Ever must we feel grief's bitter stings.

Now, now those wondrous visions of my youth
No longer are concealed.   Time's hand hath traced
In living letters all.—Swiftly they speed
Before me, one by one—and now return
In life-like form,,to tell me of the past.
—Yes, more than queen wast thou, O Josephine!
—Ah! ah!—My hammock!—Mary's voice!—The
    sea!
The sea!
—Was 't even so ?—How true to history!
Speed! Speed! My eyes do weaken—Oh I would
See all ere I depart!—'T is gone! 't is gone!—
—Again they come—but different forms—
The future—ah, the future!
Oh, tell on!
—Confusion—war—once more a throne!

        (*Apparition of* LOUIS NAPOLEON.)

                Hortense!
Hortense, behold your son!
*   .   .   .   .

Part, part your elements, etherial dome!
Bright angels, it is finished!   Bear me home !
Farewell, oh earth !   Farewell Napoleon !

                               [*Dies.*

* *See page* 154.

All withdraw except EUGENE, AUGUSTA *and* HORTENSE, *who fall on their knees by the side of* JOSEPHINE—NAPOLEON, *as before, silently regarding her.*

As JOSEPHINE'S *last words are concluded, ·the Island of St. Helena is disclosed, against which the waves are dashing, enveloped in clouds.*

The clouds are lifted, when the grave of NAPOLEON *is discovered—the spirit of the departed* JOSEPHINE *hovering over it.*

[*Curtain falls.*

---

* *The following lines may be added here, should occasion require them :*

Apparition of NAPOLEON IV.

And his!   And his!—the Fourth Napoleon!
Great France! at last your happiness has come!